Orphan Train

Charlene Oliver

Copyright © 2016 Charlene Oliver

All rights reserved.

ISBN: 1533069697
ISBN-13: 978-1533069696

**Library of Congress Control Number: 2016909890
CreateSpace Independent Publishing Platform, North Charleston, SC**

DEDICATION

First, I dedicate this book to my husband Jeff Oliver for being the glue that made me "stick" to my creative writing. His belief in me through the entire process held firm even when my belief in myself was at an end. By some strange twist of fate, his belief in me brought Brad Johnson into my life.

To Bethany, my daughter, who was my cheerleader in times of success and a shoulder to cry on when things just didn't work out.

To my daughter Jessica whose inspiration helped me never give up and the love of her life Sean Cronan.

To Chadney, my first child and her beautiful son Ian and the love of her life, Joe. She's brilliant and tough as nails.

To my mother the 'little artist' who showed me beauty and creativity through the artists hand.

To my father, a creative genius who taught me to turn my sorrow into a creative force. I miss him so much.

To Daveena, Peter and Aaron Limonick. Aaron, your inspirational art is a powerful force and I am so proud of you.
To Mary Glover and Angela who has always wanted to listen to this book.
To Max…you will never be forgotten.
And to Jeff's brother, Dennis. A rock to me and my husband even after he lost his beautiful wife Sylvia who would have loved Orphan Train.

To these people I dedicate the Love, Hope and Freedom that drives the Orphan Train.

Acknowledgments	i
Chapter One………..Warsaw, Poland, Feb 1955	3
Chapter Two……….Warsaw, Poland, Feb 1976	12
Chapter Three…….Tergovik, Poland, Nov 1940	17
Chapter Four…………………..Taken	26
Chapter Five……..………….Survival	38
Chapter Six………………..….Peter	45
Chapter Seven………….The Leaving	62
Chapter Eight………….Ravensbruck	72
Chapter Nine…………Back to Camp	96
Chapter Ten……………..……….Escape	109
Chapter Eleven…….Warsaw, Poland, Dec 1956	125
Chapter Twelve…………….Chicago, June 1976	131
Chapter Thirteen…..Warsaw, Poland, April 1957	140
Chapter Fourteen…..……New York, June 1976	146
Chapter Fifteen… ……….The Coming.	152

"Fiction cannot recite the numbing numbers, but it can be that witness, that memory. A storyteller can attempt to tell the human tale, can make a galaxy out of the chaos, can point to the fact that some people survived even as most people died. And can remind us that the swallows still sing around the smokestacks."

~Jane Yolen~

ACKNOWLEDGMENTS

Thanks go out to:

Sarah Helm (author of *Ravensbruck* which provided invaluable historical inspiration and information.

Stephen King (Author)

Natalie Goldberg (Writing Coach)

James Herbert (Author, R.I.P.)

Brad L. Johnson (Who gave my story wings and a good head wind)

Julie White (She believed in me when I didn't think I had it. She helped me believe dreams do come true. Never give up.)

ALL OF THE CHARACTERS IN THIS BOOK ARE FICTITOUS, EXCEPT THE REAL LIFE HISTORICAL FIGURES WHO LIVED THROUGH THIS AND ENTERED MY CHARACTERS LIFE ONLY IN THIS STORY. AS FOR THE REST, ANY RESEMBLANCE TO ACTUAL PERSONS, LIVING OR DEAD, IS PURELY COINCIDENTAL. ILLUSTRATIONS CREATED AND PROVIDED BY OLLY OLLY ALL IN FREE PRODUCTIONS BASED ON CHRISTINA NAVA'S SKETCHPAD.

"Monsters exist, but they are too few in number to be truly dangerous. More dangerous are the common men, the functionaries ready to believe and to act without asking questions."
~Primo Levi~

CHAPTER ONE

WARSAW, POLAND
FEBRUARY 1955

Dr. William Sherman imagined he could almost hear the grating, like shards of broken glass, tearing at his patients minds. It has been 10 years and we are not far removed from the horrors of World War II.

Still, this doctor, in his daily treatment of post-traumatic stress disorder, has been living that war through the sessions of those he tries to help. The man who sits before him now is inhabiting two lives. The 'before' and the 'after'. Who he was up until the end of the war and the man he has become. One needs redemption, the other condemnation…perhaps even death. He looks almost normal…clean shaven, chestnut brown hair streaked ever so slightly with strands of prematurely gray hairs and chiseled features. A handsome man. His dress is not of the era. A crisp white dress shirt buttoned all the way to the collar, no tie, and wide trousers. Dr. Sherman watches quietly as the man struggles to continue, twisting a small magazine until small shreds of paper float silently to the floor.

"Mr. Milner?...Jonathon ? What would you like to accomplish today? What would help you?"

The man's head snaps up. He looks startled then focuses his eyes on the doctor. He seems to relax as if he suddenly remembers where he is…and that it's not 'back then'. He speaks…quietly, "I need to tell you…I need…forgiveness".

Slumping back down in the chair he places both hands over his face.

"Mr. Milner, I have treated many survivors from the war, both military and civilian. They have gotten through this and are starting to live normal productive lives...no matter what they experienced, what they saw."

"MY pain!...My pain is deeper, it lashes out and cuts to the marrow of my bones. When I lay in bed at night and the sleep won't come, I am trapped. Like a prisoner...I go nowhere, I can talk to nobody. It is not what I saw... it is what I did. For this I am sure God will punish me...but...I...can't wait that long..," his voice trails off followed by soft sobbing.

'This is the 'after' man, repentant, needing retribution and forgiveness', the doctor thinks.

"Johnathon, what was your involvement with the war?" He asks this softly, peering closely over the reading glasses perched on the bridge of his nose, one eyebrow arched in anticipation.

But it does not appear Mr. Milner has heard the question as he speaks, "I cannot even imagine what she went through; I have to live with that...every day...every day of this cursed wretched life...beatings...cruelty...death," his words turn to mumbles.

Dr. Sherman has been taking notes but he stops now, confused, not sure of what he has heard. "What do you mean when you say 'what she went through?' Who is this you are talking about?"

Johnathon is staring at the gold carpeting, intently, his eyes following some erratic course. Dr. Sherman follows his gaze and sees an ant struggling to navigate over the clumps of material.

"Do you see this ant Mein doctor?", Johnathon asks, a bit of a German accent highlighting his words, "It's as if he is traversing a terrible terrain...I wonder if he has ever killed one of his own kind, I wonder if he feels...guilt, I wonder...", Johnathon bends over and crushes the ant with his thumb, "I wonder if he feels pain?"

The doctor recognizes the 'before' man who is speaking to him now, he wishes the "after" man would return...he does not like this one.

"Who are you?" Dr. Sherman regrets the question as soon as it has fallen from his lips.

Slowly, with a slight sneer and looking deeply into the doctors eyes he speaks, "My name is Klaus, Klaus Schuster. I was a commandant for Adolph Hitler."

The Doctor's face becomes a mask, hard and unyielding. The silence in the room is so profound he fears this man will hear the pounding of his heart. He glances around seeking refuge knowing he needs...time...time to think clearly.

"May I get you some water?" he asks, as he quickly stands and moves toward the door. No answer.

"Uh, I'll be right back", his jaw is clenched as he closes the door behind him.

In his little office kitchenette, that has served him well as he struggled to build his practice, his hands shake as he attempts to pour water into a glass tumbler. His repulsion and anger is rank and thick in the back of his throat. His eyes wander through the little door that leads to his office and caresses the image of the phone. Abruptly, he grasps the glass, spins and bolts through the door where the 'before and after man' awaits.

The Doctor has moved his chair very close and is now face to face with his patient. They are staring steadily into each other's eyes.

"Did you call them?" Johnathon asks matter-of-factly.

"Call who?"

"The authorities."

"No..", it comes out almost like a sigh from Sherman's lips, "What do you think would happen if I broke Doctor-Patient confidentiality ?"

"Become a hero?" Johnathon quips.

"Maybe," Dr. Sherman says, "but I would very likely lose my practice for violating my oath."

The doctor leans in and whispers, "I have taken care of many patients, many of whom have suffered because of who…what, you are. Frankly, it makes me want to strangle you. But no, I will not turn you in, I shall leave that to someone who has nothing to lose and merely hope and pray that it happens."

Jonathan sits up stiffly, his eyes wide and says, "So you…you will help me?"

"I will try", the doctor said, "but first, I have some questions that must be answered if we are to continue."

Johnathon nods.

"How is it that you are here? How did you manage to escape the fate that even Hitler could not?"

Slowly, Jonathan begins. He has not spoken these words to anyone…ever, "We knew the Allies were coming. Many of the soldiers under my command at Ravensbruck Camp were afraid. Many just wanted to go back home to their families. Wanted to go home as men…not murderers. Most had not, in fact, ever been in the real war. They were merely caretakers, seeing to what we believed were only 'animals. They did not want to fight. It was not their war. The war belonged to Adolf Hitler. So, many of them ran, ran off into the woods. Others laid down their guns hoping for mercy."

"And you?" the doctor asks.

"The war did not belong to me. The SS and high officials were a lot of things. Stupid they were not. We all had contingency plans, plans that had been prepared for them by an agency I will not divulge. I was relocated to Morocco long before the enemy soldiers arrived."

"I see…tell me about the woman, the 'she' you spoke of. She was a prisoner?"

"Yes", Jonathan replies and hangs his head.

"You killed her?"

"No!" Jonathan says plaintively, "Heavens no."

Realization creeps into the Doctor. "You were in love with her. You were in love with a Jew?" he asks.

"Yes...I mean, no. I was in love with a girl."

"Did she survive?"

"I believe she did, I tried to find her that last day but there was such chaos…so many dead. She is an artist. Her mother, also an artist, was very famous."

"What is her name?"

"Christina…Christina Nava. Her mother was Aurelia Navaman."

"I do not know of her mother, go on."

Jonathan is struggling, the words will not come easily, "I also believe she had a child."

"How could that have happened?" the Doctor asks, "I thought most of the babies were executed."

"Not at Ravensbruck. Many starved, many were taken but there were a few lucky ones. We had a maternity block at the camp. She had help. I think she got the baby to freedom before the war ended, before the Russians and the White Buses came."

"What has this to do with you?"

"I think I was the father." Jonathan has now collapsed into sobs.

"Good Lord!"

Dr. Sherman rises from his seat, walks to a long thin table that sits below a window. He lifts a small cedar box from it and draws out a cigarette and lights it. He begins to pace the floor trying to collect his thoughts, turns and asks, "What is it you need from me, Jonathan?"

"To listen to my story, to find some way to help me go on."

"I will listen and I will try to help you, but you should know this will not be easy and it will take time."

"I know, but it is the only choice I have."

Dr. Sherman returns to his seat, stubs out his cigarette, folds his hands over his lap…and waits.

Jonathan begins.

"I tried to find her. The Camp I was in charge of, Ravensbruck, unlike many of the thousands created by the Nazi's, housed only women. I found out later that many of the women there ended up in Tergowek, Warsaw, a small village. I purchased a home nearby and tried to seek her out. Nobody knew where she lived or even who she was. Most were suspicious of me and perhaps would not have told me even if they did know. I went through local phone books, art galleries, museums and even local art supply stores. Everything I could do without raising questions. I sought her out for the same reason I have come to you. For healing, for redemption, for a reason not to end my miserable life. I tried, more than once. But in each instance the cut was not deep enough, the pills were too few and perhaps… I just was not ready to die before I saw her again. I truly loved her."

The silence is palpable. Dr. Sherman glances at his watch and speaks, "Jonathan, I am afraid I have another patient due any time now, I will write you a prescription that should help you sleep. I am only going to give you enough to get through a few days then I want to see you next week."

CHARLENE OLIVER

"Six million of our people live on in our hearts. We are their eyes that remember. We are their voice that cries out. The dreadful scenes flow from their dead eyes to our open ones. And those scenes will be remembered exactly as they happened."

~Shimon~

CHAPTER TWO

WARSAW, POLAND
1976

The young man sat next to the bed that was occupied by a beautiful woman looking much older than her age of 51. His tape recorder is running and he waits patiently for her to speak. The news reporter scratches at his temple and flicks away a lock of ginger hair as his eyes play along the feeding tube and IV lines. She speaks, the words flow onto the thin magnetic tape twirling in his machine.

"My name is Christina Nava. My mother's name is...was Aurelia Navaman and my father's name was Frederic Amit Navaman. He changed our last name to Nava. I was born in Kosalin in Poland. It is on the outer coast, near the Baltic Sea so that makes me Polish. I have heard that I am also part French and, of course, Jewish. I will tell you now about when I was fifteen years old. This was at the time when the Nazi's had risen to power in Germany and we were horrified by what happened to the Jews there. My Momma and Poppa said not to worry, our government would never let that happen. So I believed them and did my best to be a child. But when the Nazi's invaded our country everything changed. I was young and had all the energy of a typical child that age and, oh my, I was skinny! My mother always told me I had to 'put some meat on my bones'. It wasn't for lack of trying, all I did was eat. Never gained a pound. I loved to sit by the river and try to draw like my mother. I loved the Jasper trees. I wanted to be a famous artist like my momma. I remember the first time she sold a painting. She took me to a new art store once and I begged her to buy me some of the new colors and paper but money was tight and I would have to save up from the small allowance I got. In our village people, strangers mostly, were always looking and staring at me. They were usually men. One man I remember, who worked at a bookstore, I think his name was Mr. Livermore, used to stare at me all the time. It made me feel scared. One day when my mother and I were out I saw a man staring at me. I said, Mother, why do people look at me? I don't like it. She said, 'Christina, you have been blessed with a very beautiful face. Not many girls look like you.' I told her I didn't think it was a blessing. She said, 'Christina, your face is like a work of art, it attracts the eyes of those who appreciate beauty.' Then she stopped me in front of a shop window and made me face it. 'Look at yourself, what do you see?' she asked. I said What do you mean? She repeated, 'What do you see?' I told her I didn't want to look at myself and she asked a final time, 'What do you see?' Hah! I told her, I see my face. I saw the people inside the store starting to notice me and I faced my mother and said, Mom ! Do I have to do this, it's embarrassing. She said, 'Oh don't mind them, they need to mind their own business. Christina, do you see an ugly girl in the window?' I shuffled my feet and said I don't know. 'What do you mean you don't know', she asked, 'tell me what you see.' I turned back to my reflection in the window, contemplating it and said, "Well, I see straight dark brown hair, hmmm, with streaks of lighter brown and…and…"

"Look at your eyes now, keep going."

"My eyes are green, my cheeks are chubby and my lips are big…I look like a boy with rosy cheeks and big fat lips."

"Someday," she told me, "you will be happy with your looks, I promise."

Christina fell silent, tired. The young man carefully turned off his tape machine and sat back in his chair.

"Why?" she asked, "why do you do this?"

Surprised by the question, the young man blurts out, "Well golly, that's what writers do ma'am. Find interesting stories, get all the facts and tell it to others."

Her lids are heavy but she asks, "You think my story is interesting?"

"Why…yes, I do."

"Oh my…oh my…wait until you hear the rest."

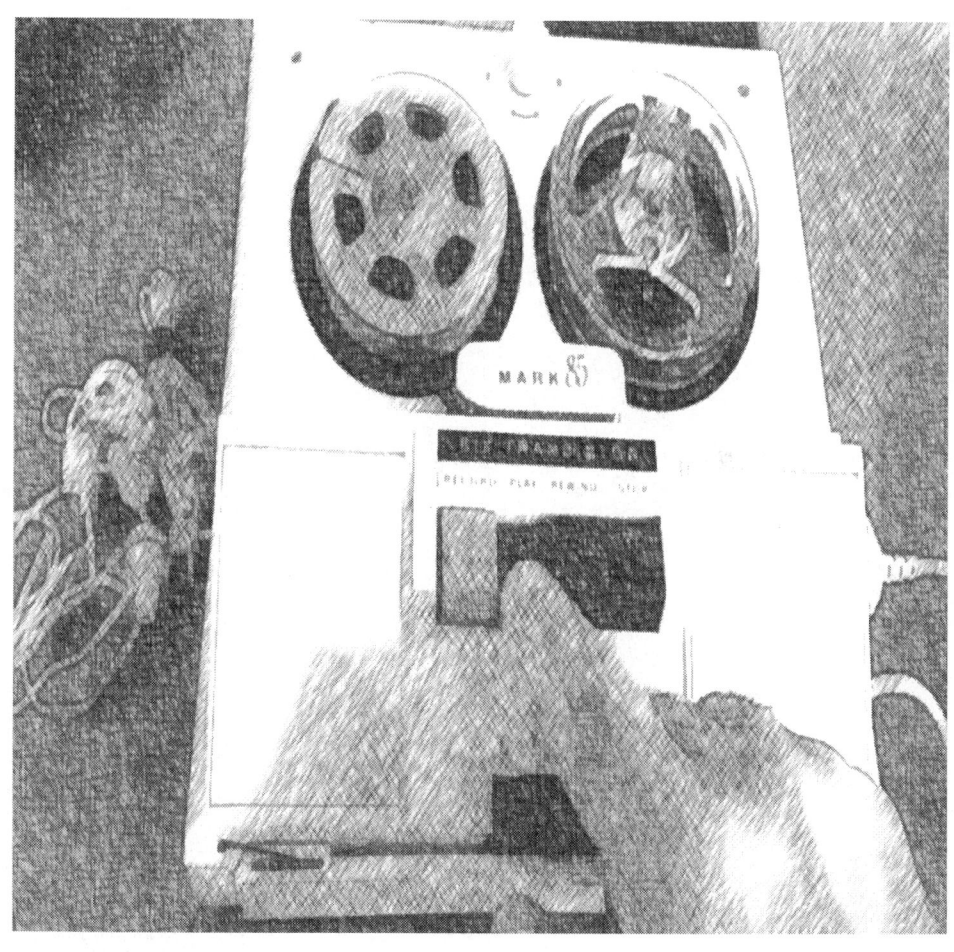

"Thou shalt not be a victim, thou shalt not be a perpetrator, but, above all, thou shalt not be a bystander"

~Yehuda Bauer~

CHAPTER THREE

TERGOVIK, POLAND

1940

A widow's veil of fog had not lifted in three days. The sun's razor edge could only scrape at it on the outskirts of the city where the forest started. The pounding of thick hands on thin doors could be heard from the street. Soldiers, arms bearing swastikas, filled hallways in the large apartment building. The Nazi's had now taken Warsaw and Poland belonged to them.

Aurelia Navaman shouted to her husband, "Frederick! Frederick! Who is that?"

"I don't know!" he said, standing in the bedroom doorway.

The pounding got louder, almost angry. Christina came out of the bathroom and asked, "What's happening?"

"It's alright, Papa will take care of it."

But she didn't think Papa looked like he wanted to, he looked scared too. Frederick Navaman walked to the door and swung the little hinged circle of brass that allowed him to see into the hall. He motions to his wife and child to go into the bedroom. Aurelia peeks around the door, slightly ajar. Frederick opens the door, ever so slightly and it bursts inward knocking him off his feet.

"What is wrong? We have done nothing, you have no right to do this!"

The big German soldier who forced his way in had dead eyes as he quickly glances around the room. There is another directly behind him looking back and forth down the hallways. His side arm has seen release from its holster. The big one makes one small step sideways and Frederick is astonished to see a very small man between them. He looks frightened too, small beads of sweat are sprinkled across his brow and he keeps pushing his little round spectacles up the bridge of his nose. He is dressed in a green vest with matching pants.

The little man speaks, in Polish, "Dockumentacja".

"Paper's?" What papers? I do not understand," Frederick replies.

"Jews!", the big soldier bellows, "You are Jews ?"

"Polish", Fredericks says, "We are Polish."

Aurelia steps out of the bedroom, walks up to the big German soldier. Christina is thinking, "My mother is very brave."

"This is our home. I will thank you to leave now. We are Polish."

It takes no effort to sweep her aside as the soldier steps over Frederick and starts pulling papers out of the small desk against the wall. He moves through the small apartment and when he is finished most of the few possessions they own are scattered across the floors. Christina has come to stand beside her mother and father, she doesn't understand.

As the soldier approaches the front door, Frederick steps up to him.

He is angry but trembling, "Are you satisfied?" The heavy meaty hand comes out of nowhere and Frederick is back on the ground, drops of blood climbing over his bottom lip and dripping onto the floor.

Frederick appeals to the small man in civilian clothes, "Please tell them we are Polish. I am sorry but we have no papers. We are citizens of this country. What are we being accused of?"

"Of being Jews, of course", the little man says as he and the soldiers leave.

From the bedroom doorway a small voice reaches out, "Momma?"

"Christina, go to bed now, everything is ok."

Christina crosses the room and hugs her mother then kneels down and kisses her father's forehead as she has done her entire life. He is still trembling. Without a word she lays down on the bed…and does not sleep, no, she listens.

"Frederick," Aurelia begins, intense with worry, "My mother was a Jew and your father was a Jew. Even though we are Polish, it is the heritage that matters."

"Do not worry Aurelia," her husband says, "I will find some papers, or get them, that says we are Polish. Things are bad enough here, we cannot go to the ghettos!"

"God will watch over us now as he always has."

Christina's parents begin to pray as they had every night. Nothing new. Perhaps, Christina thought, everything would be ok. Christina stared at the light fixture her mother had bought her when they had moved here. It had two delicate ornate roses made of white metal with crystal shimmering lights. She stared into the light and prayed, "Please keep us safe, please keep us safe."

But the questions come unbidden;

What if they come back?

What if we are arrested?

What if we are made to move to the Jewish ghettoes?

She heard her mother's voice, I have been hearing on the wireless that we will be restricted from many of our freedoms." She could not hear her father's reply but it sounded like it may have had some bad words in it.

Aurelia asked, "What are we to do then?"

"They cannot take anything from us. It is lies. All lies."

"Frederick, we need to leave."

Frederick's voice was angry, "And where are we to go? Where will I find a job? How will we live? Where will Christina go to school?"

All of these questions had no answers and Aurelia began to sob. Christina slipped from bed and marched out into the middle of the room, "Father, I will go to any school. I am scared. I think Mama is right...I think we need to leave."

Frederick pointed his finger at Christina but aimed his words at his wife, "See, see what you have started. Now we are all upset."

"But," Aurelia whispered between sobs, "we need to do something."

Frederick rose to his full height and slammed a fist onto the table, "We will do nothing! We are staying here!"

The following days were filled with warning signs. The family was asked by a friend if they would come stay with them. Of course, Frederick would not hear of it. He was, after all, a stubborn man, and proud. Aurelia told Christina it was because if they were found out the Nazi's would hurt their friends. Christina knew this was not why. One morning, in the early hours Aurelia took Christina to the bakery to get bread. The store was closed and across the window was a sign warning Non-Jews not to buy at this business owned by Jews. A large Jewish Star had been painted on the window. It was not the only sign they saw this day. Another read "Juden ist der Zutritt verboten". Aurelia told Christina it said "No admittance to Jews". Before they arrived back home, unsure of how they were to get bread, they saw a woman being pushed to the ground by soldiers.

"Mother!" Christina cried out.

"No Christina," Aurelia snapped as she grabbed Christina's arm, pulling, "Just keep walking." Christina could not even look at her mother. This was nothing like her. She cared about people. This she thought…was different.

Returning to the apartment Aurelia told Frederick what had happened. The anger rose up and he stormed from the house with his family at his heels. He was no more out the door when he ran into the old man they knew as Mordecai Bernstein. He was shaking, almost frantic.

"Have you read the papers? It is happening, all of it!"

"What are you on about old man? Move away, you are frightening my family."

"See for yourself", he said as he pushed the paper into Frederick's hands, "don't be a fool!"

Frederick unfolded the paper and began to read, headlines at first then more in greater detail. His voice started strongly but it soon became almost a whisper.

"The Jews are the reason for the trouble in our country."

Below this was a list. A list of things that were to be "verboten" for Jews to take part in:

All Driver's Licenses for Jews are hereby suspended. If you drive for a living you will have to find another job.

All Jews must be on a curfew. Curfew begins at 8:00 pm and Jews must stay in their homes until 8:00am.

Jews will not be allowed to travel outside of their resident city.

All Passports must be relinquished to Germen authorities.

Jews are hereby banned from Libraries.

Aurelia began to cry then. Christina looked up at her and said, "But Momma, if we can't go to the Library ?"

Non-Aryan doctors will no longer be able to practice medicine.

"Mother," Christina asked, "does that mean Dr. Wiesel can't take care of daddy anymore ? Daddy needs medicine."

"I, I don't know."

A small tear ran an erratic pattern down her cheek and she told Christina, "Let's go home."

Nothing more was said that morning. The silence carried over through the late afternoon and dinner. Frederick barely ate, his fork poking and moving potatoes, peas and bread around his plate. The scraping of the wooden legs of his chair across the floor startled his wife and child. Still, no one spoke. Frederick shuffled towards the bedroom, his strong shoulders seemed to droop. Christina heard him rummaging. She and her mother approached the open doorway to find him.

"What are you doing?" Aurelia asked. Frederick ignored her.

"We must leave." It was painful for Frederick to say this.

"Yes, yes, Mother…we must leave!" Christina was pulling at her dress.

As Aurelia shook her head, she said, "Didn't you read the newspaper? Our passports will be taken away…it is…too late."

Frederick did not even stop to acknowledge his wife. She said again, "It is too late. They know who we are…where we are. Frederick started yelling at Aurelia, many of the words Christina did not understand.

"Stop it! Stop it! This won't help", Christina wailed," We have to have a plan! If we can't leave…and we can't stay…we can lock ourselves in! We can nail the door shut!"

Aurelia said, "They will break it down."

"But, Mother, what if they don't?" What if they think we have left and the home is empty? Is there a place, like an attic, we can hide in?"

Frederick and Aurelia looked at each other knowing the child could be right.

"I will move the sewing stuff into the bedroom, the attic is small but we can hide there."

Frederick opened the front door and stepped out into the hallway.

"Where are you going?" Aurelia almost seemed frantic.

"I must get nails…and wood."

Dusk had come, the streaks of red across the darkening sky looked ominously like blood. Frederick had managed to attach the last of the three wooden beams across the door. Large hinges connected them to the wall and the opposing side were secured with iron clips. This would, he explained to his wife and child, prevent someone from forcing the door inward but let them leave whenever they needed to.

"Will it keep them out, Poppa?" Christina asked.

"No child," he said with a wink, "but if they think we have left perhaps they will find an easier…open door, if not, then maybe buy us time to hide."

> "Escape was not our goal since it was so unrealistic. What we wanted was to survive, to live long enough to tell the world what had happened..."
> ~Jack Werber~

CHAPTER FOUR
TAKEN

The cold wrapped around them. There would be no heat tonight. Frederick sat on a small three-legged stool fiddling with the radio dials. His search for news would be in vain, his German was poor and that seemed to be all there was. Mama sat in her chair, warmed only by a small candle to light her work as she tried to finish the sweater she was making. Christina, laying flat on the floor, was drawing. She propped herself up on her elbows then stood, walking over to her mother's side.

"It will be a beautiful sweater, Momma."

"Maybe…but I must find the end of the wool, or…or the whole thing will…unravel. You wouldn't want your sweater to look like this," she held up the tangled mess and slowly laid it on her lap.

Her eyes were distant, she had a troubled look on her face.

"No. I wouldn't be able to wear that," she giggled, "but I am sure it will be the most beautiful sweater when you are done!"

Aurelia reached over and stroked her cheek. Years later, Christina would recall that moment and realize that her mother wasn't thinking about a sweater but rather…their lives.

"Frederick, our neighbors say that we should hide our valuables."

It was a simple request but it had a profound effect on him. He was not ready. Not ready to concede to this new world, not ready to hide like a squirrel in a hole hoarding it's nuts.

"We're not going anywhere! I paid for this home and everything in it. I have worked hard all my life!"

"I know Papa," Christina cried running to him and hugging him around his waist, "but I'm scared!"

The afternoon slid by. They ate cold beans from a can and the last of the crusty bread. After Aurelia had washed the few dishes, Frederick called them into the living room.

"We must talk now," he said, his voice cold, "I have heard on the wireless that we are not to leave our homes tomorrow."

"But how will you go to work?" Aurelia asked.

"I will not."

"But Poppa, we are not Jews, you told the soldiers."

"Christina, wasn't my father, grandpa Navaman, Jewish?" he asked, "Was not your mother's mother Jewish?"

Aurelia said, "Tonight we will pray. God will protect us. God will protect us, Christina."

They hid everything they could. Floorboards were taken up, filled, and replaced. The old watch Frederick had been given by his father, jewelry and what little we had. Frederick struggled as he wadded up the few bills and stuffed them into the toe of his shoes.

"You would be better off leaving that in the flour in the canister in the kitchen," Aurelia warned.

"No, I am going to put it in my shoe!"

"What if they make you take off your shoes?"

"They may take…but they will never make me take off my shoes!"

So it went until dark. Emergency bags were packed, they practiced getting into the attic as quickly as possible.

"This is ridiculous," Frederick finally said, "I am going to bed."

At that moment the street outside was bathed in light, its beams poking through the edges around the drawn curtains.

A loudspeaker blared, "All Jews Outside!"

They moved quickly, faces stretched tight in panic. Not quickly enough, as the night was filled with the thunder of pounding fists on doors. Wooden bars buckled, nails were yanked from drywall and three Nazi's stood looking at Frederick, Aurelia and Christina, bags in hand, frozen before the now useless ladder to the attic.

"Mach schnell! Mach schnell!"

Frederick yelled, "Polish, we are Polish!" and pushed their passports into the German's hands.

The papers were slid into a messenger bag as the soldier grabbed Frederick by his shirt and threw him into the hallway. Christina went to his side and Aurelia, with all the dignity and calm she could muster, walked proudly to their side.

They joined many of their neighbors who were being jostled down the stairs, some falling, some crying. When they reached the street the pure chaos enveloped them. There were screams from across the small thoroughfare of people clinging to their possessions, trying to retain what was rightfully theirs. An elderly man, still in his pajamas was yelling into the face of a Nazi, "You cannot do this!"

The soldier next to him raised his arm, the swastika glaring at Christina. At the end of that arm was a pistol. He shot the man in the head. The old man's wife screamed and dropped the cuckoo clock she was carrying. The soldier who had killed her husband crushed it beneath his boot. Most of the people froze, silenced by the reality and brutality. Christina could not watch, she buried her face in her mother's dress.

"How can they do this?" Aurelia asked her husband.

"Just keep quiet, for God's sake keep quiet!".

They huddled in small groups, surrounded by soldiers with guns aimed at them. No one moved, no one spoke as the other soldiers brought keepsakes, momentos and anything that might be of value and threw them into the street.

A German soldier of some higher rank it seemed came out of their building. In his hands he carried two of Aurelia's paintings.

One was a moonlit forest in the dead of a harsh winter featuring a small clearing with a light blanket of snow. Three dear could be seen next to a tree with no leaves. The other, a scene of a Polish farmer in front of a thatch covered house pulling water from a well to quench the thirst of two horses as his wife looked on. She wore a bright red scarf on her head with her hand on her hip and a smile on her face.

"Who painted this ?"

"I did, I did" Aurelia said in a strong voice and without thinking, "I am an artist. If you would like I will paint one for you."

A few of the soldiers gathered around, each looking at the paintings that had garnered the interest of their commander. The painting of the farmer was not finished. Christina had always hoped that when she was as good an artist as her mother, she would let her complete it. She would paint the soft purple and pink petals indicating Spring was coming, new life…and hope. The truth of life. She didn't feel that now. The commander held the painting at arm's length and dropped it onto the street, pulled the ugly black Luger pistol from his hip and blasted several bullet holes into it. Christina gasped, feeling a bit of her soul being ripped out of her.

"Quiet." Her mother said.

She was squeezing her tightly. Her father put his head down low, unable to look anymore.

Under his breath, Frederick whispered, "We have our family…together…that is all that matters now."

Christina looked up at the building across the street and saw her friend, Mathilda, in the window her mother behind her with both hands placed gently on her shoulders. They were both crying. Christina wondered, as they, and many of their neighbors were being led down the cobblestoned road, why were they crying? They didn't have to leave their homes…they were not Jews. If all the people who were not Jews did something…anything, maybe they could stay.

The dawn had come but it was bitter cold. They had been walking for quite some time and Frederick was sure they were being taken to the train station. Christina noticed that the more and more often those ahead of them who trying to carry as many of their valuables as possible began to drop them by the wayside. It was too far, they were too heavy. Photographs, trinkets, expensive rugs, paintings , even clothes littered the street as the march continued. Behind them a loud disturbance erupted and grew in intensity. There were shouts and screams and it was rapidly approaching them. Frederick stood on his tip toes and a flash of horror streaked across his face. The crowd was splitting in two like a flimsy piece of cotton being torn...and it was headed directly for them.

"Get down!" he yelled at his wife and child, "get to the curb!"

A middle-aged lady rushed by them quickly followed by several soldiers. The first caught the back of her coat and spun her around. With no hesitation he placed the blackened end of his pistol to her forehead and pulled the trigger. The crowd fell into a deathly silence. A thin framed man broke through the crowd and fell to his knees at the dead woman's side crying, "Mama! Mama!"

From above they heard the cries of those who had not been torn from their homes, those that were not Jews. They were spitting on them, yelling, "Damn You! Damn you Jews!" The woman in front of them vomited and they were forced to tramp through it as the crowd around them was unyielding.

Christina felt her mother's arm surround her, draping over her shoulder and pulling her into her side. The only thought that filled her head was, 'When will I turn around and find a gun, pointed at me or at my mother and father? Will we become just another body laying dead in the street like that woman?'

She didn't know anything anymore. Her thoughts dwelled only upon the people she loved and the people who loved her. The thoughts that became a looming shadow in her should not be those of the young. They are not ready and perhaps may never be ready, even as adults. Life is a gift, these things were happening are transgressions on the soul. When you see people, innocent people, ordinary people shot for no reason, it's then that the shadows come, like a beast. It is a black hole pulling you into the darkness of sorrow. At that moment, when you know for sure that life will never be the same, it is then when you must grasp out, reaching for anything that will pull you up from the darkness.

Christina had to keep pulling herself up from that darkness. She tried. The dark pit that yawned before her, in her mind, seemed too large. She sought the strength her father always told her she had. She was feisty and headstrong he had said, and she had to stay that way. Questions flooded into her mind, legitimate questions like: 'Why is this happening? Why do we have to be punished? Why us?'

She knew then that she could not, would not, allow these monsters to take the one thing that was worth living for: her freedom, her hopes and her dreams. The real question was what could she do? Protest? Did she think they would listen to her? Yes, like they listened to the woman with the bullet in her head lying dead in the street? I am nobody, she thought, just a young girl. They will shoot me.

As this last thought lingered in her they approached a frail man addressing a soldier. He was so polite and kindly asked the man if perhaps he could just sit on the sidewalk for moment…to rest…to ready himself for the journey and keep up with the rest.

"Yes, you may rest" the soldier said as he shot him in the face, "rest."

Christina screamed, and her mother grabbed her, placing her hand over her eyes. she sunk down to another level of fear and trepidation called on that feistiness, her father told me her she had, and it was not there. Instead, her mind found a new place to be. She was nine years old and listening to her mother humming her favorite melody. She didn't know where it was from, but it was beautiful and haunting, and when she was humming, she was happy. She found herself sitting on the front porch with her easel, painting the Koszalin hills, covered with lilies and silver white snow on the mountain peaks. She found it brought her a feeling of peace and freedom. These two things were the most precious in life.

She remembered her mother doing portraits for friends and even strangers and she was becoming more and more famous throughout Koszalin. She was best known for her drawings of the hills and the meadows of Koszalin and Poland. Poland was so beautiful. There were castles and farms, and the meadows were stunning.

Her mother said to her, "Christina, I pray that one day you will be filled with the passion to paint, and I pray your children as well as their children, will also have the passion to paint…to seek out peace and freedom in it."

She said, 'But mother, I don't know what I want to do.'

'One day Christina. One day you will know,' she said, taking her hands in hers and speaking in her thick Polish accent, 'Christina, don't you let these hands, or this heart, go to waste. Remember what your heritage is. I have prayed to God that the gift of art will find you. It is God's purest form of all life's expression.'

Christina replied smiling, 'But mother, if I do paint, I would want to be as good as you.'

Aurelia said, "One day, you will. Christina, I know you will, and when you do, my beautiful daughter, paint the sky. The sky is freedom."

She looked deep in her eyes; folded her hair back behind her ear and said, "Freedom is for your heart and your soul. It is the only gift that can never be taken away from you. It is in the hand of the artist where God expresses his love to the world."

She lifted up a large black artist's case and added, "Maybe one day you can finish this painting." She started to pull out a canvas, than she put it back in its case, replying, "No, not now."

Christina said, "What is it, mother?"

"You'll find out Christina, you'll find out. It is one on my favorite pieces, but it is unfinished. Maybe one day you will finish it for me."

She hugged her, saying, "I would love that mother."

That thought would stay with her even to this horrible day. She stepped on a jagged pebble, jarring her back from peaceful place of solace.

They had been walking for a long time and Christina tried to imagine her father's feet. They must be hurting him so badly. They all had to follow the mass of people, as they were guided into an area, where brick walls were being built.

They passed a soldier. He looked as though he might be in his early twenties. Christina thought he was handsome. She couldn't understand why someone like him could be brainwashed to kill innocent people. Didn't he have a girlfriend or a life? These questions would remain forever unanswered.

He was standing in front of what looked like an old apartment building, with unpainted iron bars bolted to the windows and right next to it, a small chemist with broken windows and scattered supplies on the floor. The soldier was holding onto a large weapon, yelling at the top of his lungs. Christina couldn't understand him but he kept waving his hands, signaling for them to come, come, come.

They walked towards him and then, for no reason, one of the other soldiers behind them shoved Frederick so hard, it caused him to fall to his face.

Christina shouted, "Father!," and ran to him, but the young soldier grabbed her by the arm. Her mother froze. He pulled out his sidearm, putting it to her temple and looked deep into her horrified eyes. There was a moment deathly silence and Christina could only think of one thing…she smiled at him.

He slowly took the gun away from her head and released her. She ran to her father. He was bleeding from his cheek.

Her father scolded, "What are you thinking, you fool girl? Don't ever do that again!"
She struggled to help him to his feet. It was then that they were introduced to their new home. It was horrible and, as with so many others, she hated it.

She said, "Mother, what is this place? "
Her mother did not answer. Christina did not understand. As they filed through the iron gate and were led down the small street filled with ugly buildings, the people ahead of them were pushed through doorways as a guard counted them. This area of town was mostly industrial, small, squat and dingy. In this ghetto there were far too many people. They learned later they would to be forced to live 12, 13, even as many as 16 in a unit.

They weren't even apartments. Mostly, they were office buildings with one or two dozen large empty rooms, one bathroom and a kitchenette break room. When the order came to move here many objected…and many died. They learned later that Reinhard Heydrich, a high ranking German in the Nazi party, had a plan. If a community had 500 or less Jews they were rounded up and shipped to the ghettos. In larger Jewish populated areas they were told to stay and all non-Jews were forced to move. Soon after, these ghettos were filled beyond their capacity to function. All ghettos were isolated from the world by walls or chain link fences topped with barbed wire. All the gates had armed guards. The gates of tears were the only ones unlocked.

"Part of her revolted against the insanity of the rules. Part of her was grateful. In a world of chaos, any guidelines helped. And she knew that each day she remained alive, she remained alive. One plus one plus one.. The Devil's arithmetic...."

~Jane Yolen~

CHAPTER FIVE

SURVIVAL

The door on the second floor of the building they were directed into creaked. There was a rank of filing cabinets against the wall to the right of the room and, on the far left side, windows faced the street. Butcher paper had been taped to the windows. A broken table, occupied the center of the room. There were no chairs, no cots and no beds.

A pile of old musty blankets had been thrown into the corner. There was one bathroom on this floor at the end of the hall.

They would have to line up and take turns to use the toilet. It didn't matter how badly one would have to go, they would have to wait, and it seemed with as many others that would be living here it would be constantly occupied.

It was the most humiliating and disgusting situation Christina could have ever imagined. There were as many as 4 other families who would be living in this small room with them. There were also a few stragglers, who just seemed to keep showing up. They told them that they could not live in the street and the other buildings had even more people. They begged them to let them stay and most refused them until they claimed to have an idea of where they could get extra food.

Frederick addressed the others, "They can stay as long as the Germans don't find out that they have left their other living quarters. No trouble, there must be no trouble."

One of them said, "We didn't have any living quarters".

"Okay," Frederick said, "find a spot, but, I will not have you putting my family in danger. Do you understand?"

They answered, "We understand."

One of the men kept looking at Christina. He was an older man. She didn't like him. He was dirty, smelled and looked like a "wloczega", a bum.

She asked her father, "Why do those men have to live here with us? Why don't they leave? They are making me nervous."

Her father answered, "Don't worry Christina! I told them to mind their own business."

She pleaded, "But Father, one of the men keeps looking at me and he smells."

Frederick said, "Don't worry. Just ignore him."

She tried but he seemed to know that he intimidated her and he took advantage of the situation.

As the light filtering in through the blocked window began to fade, the smelly man would make whispering sounds, pursing and licking his lips whenever she glanced at him. She turned away after giving him a dirty look, but he wouldn't stop and so Christina went to her father and said, "Father, that one man is making sounds at me and sticking out his tongue."

Frederick stopped what he was doing and looked across the room. The man was staring at him with a smirk on his face. He walked over to the man, very close, and whispered, "Stop making eye contact with my daughter and stop making sounds at her. If you don't stop, you will have to leave."

The man slowly put his hands in his pockets but did not respond.

Frederick said, "Do you understand?" His hands were at his side balled into fists.

"Yes," the man said quietly.

Frederick said, "I didn't hear you."

"Yes" the man said louder, before turning away.

Frederick walked back over to where his family had lain down a blanket and sat down.

As evening fell, they did the best they could to be as comfortable as possible. A lot of the younger teens were sitting in a circle talking about what they had seen and cursing the German soldiers. Some of them had brought cushions so they would be more comfortable, while the elderly were forced to lie on the cold hard floor.

"It's horrible." Christina said to one boy. "Why don't you give the soft cushion to the older people?"

"No." He snapped back.

Her father said, "Christina, don't worry."

"But father," she pleaded, "You must be hurting."

"No, I'm fine." he answered, "Just lie down and get some rest."

She got herself as comfortable as she could folding the blanket to put as much padding between her small frame and the cold hardwood floor. All three Nava family members had brought the small rucksack each had packed for themselves when they had planned their escape to the attic. They were using them now for pillows. After a few hours, Christina could not wait any longer, she had to go to the toilet, but she was afraid. In the dark she could not see the man that was making sounds at her, but it didn't matter she couldn't hold it any longer. She got up slowly and very quietly tiptoed, looking over her shoulder every second. She entered the bathroom, closing the door and then she lowered her head, whispering, "Thank you God."

After she finished she opened the door, and the doorway was filled with the man she had hoped to avoid. Before she could even pull a breath to scream, he grabbed her throat and mouth and shoved her back into the bathroom. He threw her to the floor, and grabbed at her shorts trying to pull them down. Christina tried to scream, but he said, "If you scream, I will cut your throat. I suppose we are all going to die anyway." He pressed a sharp object against her throat. She kept very still.

He said, "Good girl." As he unzipped his pants, Christina slapped him as hard as she could, right across the face, knocking him backward as he lost his balance. Christina jumped to her feet, both hands balled into fists just as someone banged on the door, yelling, "Open up!" It was a woman, yelling, "Open the door, now!"

The man jumped up and ran out, knocking the woman to the ground. She hissed at him and Christina saying, "Well! I never." The woman forcefully pushed her way into the bathroom as Christina slid out the door. She was hurting and frightened, and somehow feeling guilt and shame. She didn't tell her mother or father what had happened. She curled herself into a ball and lay quietly between her parents.

In the morning light she looked around to see where the man had gone, but he was gone and she never saw him again.

A short time later they heard a commotion down the hall as the soldiers barged into the rooms. When their door flew open the young German soldier that had held a gun to Christina's head just yesterday threw a wad of yellow material, a small sewing kit and a pair of dull scissors on the floor. He was followed by an older lady who spoke to them in Polish and ordered them to cut yellow stars and sew them onto their clothing. Aurelia carefully gathered up the material and began cutting stars from it. They learned the yellow material was only for the Jews and if you didn't wear a yellow star, you would be severely punished or killed, depending on the mood of the soldier who saw them.

Some refused to wear them.

Some of the last to arrive had heard on the wireless that the German troops had penetrated the Hungarian territories.

Frederick said, "That is a very bad sign."

Everyone was becoming angry and losing their tempers. There was one man who became extremely hostile. He would enter the bathroom, slam the door, and say, "Stay out of my room!"
A man sitting on the far side of the room scurried to the commotion, pushed the door open and said, "This is not your room. It belongs to all of us."
Some of the younger women began to clean, tearing away the butcher paper to let light in then scrubbing the windows with water from the toilet. There were many women, both younger and a few older, but only a few older men. This made Christina feel uncomfortable, where she wondered, were all the men?

"If you had to pack your whole life into a suitcase-not just the practical things, like clothing, but the memories of the people you had lost and the girl you had once been-what would you take?"

~Jodi Picoult~

CHAPTER SIX

PETER

The days were long, the nights even longer. The little bit of food they had managed to bring with them was gone. The Germans had only brought bits of bread and a gray slop they called soup. No one felt safe, few ventured out at all.

All Christina wanted to do was get swallowed up into her artwork, at least she had her pad and pencils for her sketching. She was sitting on the balcony in the front of the building allowing the elderly to sit in the battered chairs they had found, seeking out the sun. She noticed the walls where they had entered that first day had gotten higher. Some of the older folks would try to explain why they were building them, some said to keep us in, some said to protect them from the rest of the Poles who thought the Jews had wrecked their country and turned the Nazi's against them. Nobody could agree, until a woman came running into the lounge, shouting at her husband, "Look here, look. It shows the district we are living in."

She glided a gnarled finger over the paper, "See the walls? They are to keep us separated from everyone else. The sections we are in are only for the Jews and anyone who is seen going beyond the limits will be killed, but there are thousands of us. How can we all live here? It is impossible. It is only a 6-block area," She paused and then continued, "We will never be released." The woman started to sob.

A man screamed at her saying, "Shut up. They will not keep us here. They will send us to Lodz, maybe. There over 160 thousand there but at least they have apartments."

She turned, with tears streaming down her red face and said, "Yes they can. See for yourself."

The man snubbed her and said, "The Americans will come and they will help us."

Another man responded bitterly, "The Americans help? You must be joking. No, they won't. They will not come near this place. They say, 'It is not their war. It is Germany's war.'"

The man turned back, tending to his shoes, mercilessly shining them. There was another man who had a small wireless radio. His ear was glued to it, every minute of every day, trying to listen for the latest update on what was happening. There were always a few who stayed close to him. One said, "If you are caught with that radio, they will kill you. They took mine away."

The man answered, "Well, they will not take this." The man grunted and walked away tucking his radio under his arm.

Christina pulled on her coat with the yellow star sewn on it. She had to get out, walk around and listen to what the others were saying. Maybe she could spend a little bit of the change she had. She would love some sweets. She went to tell her mother, but she was too busy tending to her father. She walked outside thinking he was looking sick again.

As she walked out the door, she did hear her mother's voice say, "Christina, what is it you want?"

But she didn't answer her. She knew she should have, but she thought she might have told her to stay in. That would never do. The streets were crowded. There were many soldiers and people walking in aimlessly. People were shoving others for no reason.

Some were on the sidewalk, their backs against the brick walls…begging for food. She couldn't bear to watch this.

She came upon a small grocery store. She walked in and looked but there was no food here. She just wanted some chocolate, or anything sweet. A man hurried around the counter, glaring at her. She looked at him, smiling.

He said, "What do you want?" He was still glaring at her.

She said, "I would like to buy a chocolate bar."

He said, nothing. He threw back his head and laughed. She thought maybe he hadn't heard her and she asked again, "Sir, may I buy…"

She wasn't able to finish her sentence, when he yelled, "Get out of here."

She stood frozen, shock drifting across her young face. No one had ever yelled at her like that, even when she was in trouble with Father. She apologized, "I am sorry sir, but I only want to buy a bar of Chocolate."

He yelled, " You can buy nothing. Any money you have is worthless, now get out. Didn't you hear me?"

He spit on the ground at her feet, and said, "All you people are the same. You steal and run like cowards and take what is not yours. Now get out. GET OUT OF HERE!"

She left the store crying and ran back as fast as she could. She didn't want her mother to see the tears, she wiped her face on her sleeve. She could hear her mother yelling. She went into the kitchenette and said, "Mother what happened? What is wrong?"

"This woman has accused me of taking rice that doesn't belong to me."

Looking at the heavy set woman Christina asked, "You accused my mother of stealing?"

She didn't wait for an answer but saw the pitifully small bag of rice in woman's hands and said, "We brought it from home."

The woman screamed, "Of course you are going to say that. You are a liar too! Now you leave it alone, and get out of my way."

Aurelia looked at her and said, "Come on, Christina. Leave her alone."

"But mother."

She put her hand on her daughters shoulder and said, "Come on."

They walked into the other room and Christina asked, "Why did you let her do that to us? You know that rice was ours."

Her mother gritted her teeth and answered, "What am I supposed to do Christina, hit her or grab it from her?"

"Why didn't you ask Father to help you?"

Her mother looked at Christina, exhausted, "Have you seen him lately?" she sighed, "He can't even help himself."

Christina spoke and it broke her mother's heart, "But mother, I am so hungry."

Her mother said, "I know, I know you are dear. We are all hungry."

Aurelia, who didn't have a mean bone in her body, turned looking in the direction of where the woman was and said, "And I hope they choke on it."

They started to laugh uncontrollably. Their legs grew weak as they collapsed onto the floor, laughing hysterically, but soon the laughter turned to tears and then sobs. Mother and daughter wrapped themselves in each other's arms. Aurelia wiped her face and Christina's and then said, "Don't let your father see that you have been crying."

Christina said, "I know. He would never believe me if I told him I was crying because I was laughing so hard."

Aurelia then changed the subject and said, "I will have to send father out to get something."

"No mother. Father can't go. He is so weak."

Aurelia said, "It is too dangerous for either of us to go. It has to be a man."

Christina was insistent, "Maybe we can ask one of the other men to go for us."

Her mother replied, "You must be kidding. They wouldn't even give up a seat for you or me. They would never go out for us."

"But mother, I was kicked out of a store today. The store owner thought I was going to steal from him."

"Kicked you out! Are you all right?"

"Yes I am fine. My feelings were the only thing that was hurt."

Aurelia said, "Many people are very angry and say things they don't mean. Maybe if your father goes, they will not think he is going to steal food because he is older."

Christina responded, "But I saw another lady being thrown to the ground and she was older. It is terrible. What is happening? I don't understand!"

Her mother wiped her eyes and reassured her, "Christina, this will all be over, don't worry."

"But why? Why are we held here like this? I don't understand this kind of hatred. Is it really because we are Jewish? Is that why?" Her mother didn't answer her so she continued, "That is pretty stupid. They don't even know me. We are just like them."

Her mother turned and harshly said, "We are nothing like them. Never say that again. I don't want to hear another word about it. Now find a place to sit down, while I figure out what we are going to eat."

She had never known her mother to be so angry. She sat down on the floor in the living quarters and feel asleep.

Two hours passed and she woke up feeling stiff. As she adjusted her clothing and caught something from the corner of her eyes, someone looking at her. It was a boy in the corner of the room; he was sitting in a chair, a comfortable chair and she wondered where on earth he had gotten it. He was smiling at her. Christina immediately looked back down and fumbled with her drawing and pencils. She dared a glance toward the boy. He was looking directly at her, still smiling. This was a different smile than she had seen in the last few days from men. It didn't scare her or seem creepy. That thought alone let her return the smile. The boy mouthed, "Do you want to sit here?"

She pointed her finger at herself and mouthed back, "Are you talking to me?" He nodded yes.

She looked around, there were so many people lying on the cold floor, old people, young people, then she looked back and nodded yes and gathered up her materials, stood and walked over to him.

Looking around, she said, "Thank you, would you mind if I give the chair to that old woman. She pointed, "She has been crumpled up on the floor for hours. Is that okay?"

"Yes that is fine," he said, "but I am offering it to you. If you choose to give it to her, that is your choice."

"Yes, I would like to do that."

He said, "But if I get up, and you aren't sitting in the chair, somebody else will grab it."

Christina said, "Okay." She wasn't sure what he wanted her to do.

"Here," he said, "You sit here and stay. Don't move a muscle."

She quickly sat down. Many eyes were on her, as if she held a piece of meat for starving animals.

An old man said, "Please, can I have that seat?"

Another voice, a woman pleaded, "Please, give me your seat."

The heavy built woman who had stolen their rice said, "I want that seat! Now get up."

She charged at Christina with full force, throwing herself against the chair. Christina held on. The woman continued to scream, "Give me the chair."

The chair was rocking and rocking. Christina was sure it was going to tip over. She hollered, "Help me!"

The boy, who was assisting the old woman to her feet, came over, grabbing the woman, who was throwing herself against Christina and said, "Stop it! This chair is for this woman."

There was a murmur of complaints, as he escorted the older woman to the chair.

She looked up at him, eyes filled with disbelief, but so much compassion and said, "Thank you dear, thank you." She looked at Christina and said, "thank you," then she kissed her hand as a sign of respect. Christina smiled back at her and she kissed her hand to return the gesture.

Christina returned to the floor and the boy followed, sitting next to her. She turned to him and shyly commented, "That was kind of you to offer your seat to me."

He replied, "Maybe, but It was much kinder for you to offer the seat to that woman. Anyone else would have taken it for themselves, but she is much older than most of them. I think I'm looking at an angel."

He smiled and at that moment, Christina realized he was incredibly handsome.

"Thank you," she replied, chuckling, "But I'm no angel."

He asked her, "How long have you been here?"

She said, "Probably as long as you have."

He asked, "Are your parents here?"

"Yes. I am here with my mother and father. Are you with your parents?"

"I am here only with my mother."

She said, "Did you hear the argument that was happening in the kitchen?"

"Yes I did. Is everything all right?"

"No. We are not thieves."

The boy said, "Was it your rice? Because if it was not I could under...."

She cut him off, "Of course it was our rice. My mother would never steal anything! It wouldn't matter how hungry she was, she would never steal."

She turned away from him annoyed and opened her pad of drawings.

"What are you drawing?" he asked leaning over, trying to see what was in her book.

"I draw what I see." she said.

"What do you see here?" The boy said.

"I see people, lonely people, sad people, angry people but mostly forgotten people."

He looked at her with mild amusement and then said, "You're a pretty negative girl, aren't you?"

"I'm not negative."

"Yes you are." He laughed, turning towards me, "But who can blame you? There is only sadness here."

She didn't answer. She knew he was right.

Christina said, "I see people, young ones who should not have this happen to them…and old people who never have. We all have a soul and it doesn't matter where we were or how we lived, rich, poor or in between. See that man in the corner with the funny hat? He was my father's doctor. He lived in the nicest house we ever saw. But he is here now, living like we are. It doesn't matter how we got here. We are all together and I believe we all have a new destination in this life. We have to believe in something. We have to have faith." She caressed her pad of sketches, "This…this is my faith."

He sat there for a while, then said, "Do you have anything I can see?"

"Yes." She flipped over the paper and showed him her Jasper trees.

He said, "That is wonderful, I mean, beautiful." He looked deep into her green eyes. "How long have you been drawing?"

"Since I was just a little girl."

He said, "Do you have anymore?"

"Yes." She turned to the next page; it was a drawing of an old man praying.

He said, "Who is he?"

She answered, "I really don't know. I have may have dreamt of him. He is always in the same position when I think of him, praying."

The boy asked, "Do you pray?"

"Yes, I do. Do you?"

The boy looked uncomfortable, "Sometimes, but I never seem to get an answer. I didn't introduce myself. My name is Peter. What is yours?"

"My name is Christina."

"Good to meet you Christina." He held out his hand formally and she shook it.

"Nice to meet you too." She liked the way he had said her name. She liked the warmth of his hand in hers. She remembered just how he said it and let it bounce around her memory, 'Christina…..Christina.'

She thought again how handsome he was. She liked his blue eyes and short blond hair.

She asked, "How old are you?"

He said, "I am seventeen years old. How old are you?"

"I am turning fifteen on the seventeenth of October."

He said, "My birthday is in October too, but I am on the 3rd. Could you draw me?"

She was afraid of what her face revealed, that he would see that she would love to draw that face. She didn't even know him. The fact that he gave her his seat and that he looked her deep in her eyes, she kinda thought she would just melt. His eyes, he had beautiful eyes. She realized she was sitting there…staring while he was waiting for an answer

"Yes, of course, I will."

She realized in that moment she wanted to kiss him. Wanted to reach over and kiss him, but she wasn't going to do that…no, she would feel like a fool.

"Sit down over there," she said.

He scooted over to the side of the chair that the woman was sitting on and Christina started to draw.

There was a woman nearby watching her. She was studying her as she was trying to capture Peter's face. His features were perfect. She was getting all giddy as she was sketching his full mouth. He had the most beautiful lips she had ever seen.

The woman edged a bit closer watching and then she interrupted the silence, saying,

"You are very good."

"Thank you." Christina said.

Peter said, "Let me see."

"No, not yet."

She spent a bit more time giving the drawing a finishing touch and then turned the drawing pad towards Peter. He couldn't stop staring at it and finally said, "Christina you are amazing. How did you learn to draw like that?"

She said, "My mother was a very good artist. Do you really like it?"

Peter leaned over and kissed her on the cheek. She felt the fire blazing up from her neck and shuddered. She wanted to kiss him back so badly, but this was her first kiss and she didn't know where to start. The tingles that were all over her body seemed to know exactly what to do, but she was too shy.

The light had dimmed in the room, the shadows were long but Christina continued to draw as Peter lay beside her, feet crossed and hands behind his head. She shifted trying to get more comfortable and realized her legs and butt were numb. Peter was asleep next to her. She turned around to look at the little lady that they had given the chair to, but there was a man sitting there instead.

She shook Peter and said, "Peter, wake up! Someone else is sitting in the chair."

Peter stirred a bit and she rose to her feet. Everything hurt; her legs were stiff. Christina walked over to the man and said, "Where is the woman, who was here?"

The man said nothing offering only a shrug.

She said again, "Where is she?"

He said in a small voice, "She is over there."

The woman was laying on the floor, in the fetal position. She went over to her, trying to wake her, "Ma'am? Ma'am?" She shook her, "Ma'am. Are you all right?"

Still she didn't answer.

"Ma'am." Christina said louder. Peter had gotten up.

She said, "Peter. Please help."

Peter went over the man, who was in her seat and said, "What did you do?"

He said, in his weak voice, "She was dead, so I just took her seat."

Christina came over and said, "Did you push her onto the floor?"

He said, "No she just fell." The man started to cry, "I didn't touch her. I swear."

Christina said, "You liar."

Another voice behind them said, "He is telling the truth. She died, she fell and he took her seat."

Christina looked at the man in the chair and said, "I am sorry." She placed her hand on the man's shoulder and repeated, "I am sorry......sir."

She turned and grabbed onto Peter's shirt staring in horror at the still body on the floor and cried, "So now what do we do? We can't just leave her here."

A woman with a cold hard voice said, "Just leave her there. The soldiers will take her away."

Christina and Peter sat back down on to the floor together, but in a different spot. Christina dosed off in Peter's arms and after about an hour, she opened her eyes and watched the final light of day slip away. She couldn't bear to look at that poor woman crumpled up on the floor.

The next morning, Christina awoke to moaning and crying. Two men, one her father's doctor and another she did not know, were wrapping the dead woman in a blanket.

A man saw looking at her and said, "The soldiers would not take her. They said to tend to our own kind."

Her mother came over to her. Christina thought she looked so very tired. She said, "Mother. Are you all right?"

No answer came.

Christina took her hand and said, "Sit down with me?"

Aurelia said, "Don't worry about me. I am fine. It's your father I'm worried about."

Fear framed Christina's face and she asked, "Where is he?"

Aurelia said, "He's in the lounge and he does not look well. He is getting weaker and weaker. We have to do something about food. We are going to starve if we don't find something."

Peter overheard the conversation and said, "Wait here. I will be right back." He got up and went into another room.

Her mother sat on the floor with her, slowly stroking her hair and said, "He looks like a nice boy. What is his name?

Christina said "His name is Peter."

They could hear Peter talking. He was speaking quietly to his mother, than she heard, "You can give them this much. This much only!"

Peter said, Thank you mother." He came back a few minutes later and said, "Here, My mother said you can have this." He handed Aurelia a brown paper bag.

"I know it's not a lot and I wish we had more…"

She opened it and said, interrupting, "It's enough, thank you. Thank you so much, please tell your mother I say thank you so very much. Christina, give some to your father so he can regain some of his strength."

Peter said, "I must go. It's time for my medication."

Christina said "What medication?"

Peter said, "It tastes awful, but I need it every day. I have a sickness and if I don't treat it, it could would be very bad. It doesn't matter, the medicine is almost gone."

"What do you have?" Aurelia asked.

"I don't really know. My mother told me once, it has a long funny name, but I don't remember. It doesn't matter, the medicine is almost gone and it does not seem anything will change that."

Peter looked into Christina's eyes and said, "Everything is fine, do not worry, I have you as my friend now."

Christina couldn't help but let a smile flash across her face. But she was worried.

Peter gave her a peck on the cheek and said, "Christina, don't you realize, if we weren't here, I never would have met you?"

Aurelia arched her eyebrow and said, "That sounds like something you have read in a romantic novel."

"No. I mean it."

Aurelia slowly rose to her feet and said," I am going to check on your father."

Christina started to aimlessly sketch on her pad. Peter could see a slight blush on her neck.

"Peter, you hardly know me."

"I feel like I have known you forever," he said.

"So answer this smarty-pants, what do you think is my favorite color?"

He had a quizzical look on his face and said, "Well, your hair is brown, and your eyes are green."

She interrupted him, "That's easy, what do you think my favorite color is?"

There was a bit of an uncomfortable pause and he then replied, "I think your favorite color is yellow, like wildflowers, and like the sun."

Christina didn't really have a favorite color but she said, "You are right, my favorite color is yellow, it is the color of life."

Peter said, "I must go and take my medicine."

He gave her another peck on the cheek. He was gone for over an hour and she was thinking about him, and then she heard him coming down the stairs and he didn't look good.

She asked, "Are you all right?"

He said, "Yes, I am fine."

He sat back down next to her, and she sat back, sinking deep into the cradle of his arm. She was as comfortable as she had ever remembered. The awful place they were in faded around her. She was afraid she was feeling love for the first time with this boy and now, more than ever wishing things were different. Could this really be a place to fall in love?

Peter then said something that made her realize he was not just handsome, he was smart as well.

"Does it matter Christina if we are here? If we are laughing or crying?"

She had a puzzled look on her face and said, "What do you mean?"

He said, "Is there really any difference? All the emotions that we feel? As long as we can have this? He gave her a gentle squeeze.

She said, "Peter, you have such a beautiful way of seeing things."

She stopped a moment, frowned and continued, "But there is so much suffering here. A woman just died in the next room and I am so hungry. My stomach is no longer growling, it is roaring, and I feel hollow and sick."

Peter said, "I can hear it."

She grabbed her stomach with embarrassment, and said, "No you can't." She looked up at him, smiling, "Well, I can hear your stomach too."

Peter said, "I don't think I have a stomach anymore."

He started to laugh and she joined him. After a few minutes, he teased, "Can you hear what it is saying?"

"Let me see." She put her head to his belly and said, "All I can hear is a rumble and a gurgle."

He said, "It is saying you are so pretty and I think I love you."

She lifted her head off of his stomach and said, "Did you just say you love me?"

There was an awkward pause before he said, "Yes. I did."

She turned, facing him and said, "But really you don't even know me. This is not a place for love, Peter. It is a place where people fight for chairs, and where children and teenagers steal, and where people are crying, and we hear guns being fired. A whole race of people are being starved and killed. There is something terrible happening and my father is sick."

She stopped and a small sob escaped.

Peter touched her face and said, "But I know me…and I know how I feel."

"Peter, do you really think that I am pretty?"

He said, "You're a funny girl."

"Oh, is that good or bad?" she asked.

He looked at her and she thought, 'I would never have asked a boy that. Never!'

Peter said, "Christina. Have you ever been kissed? I mean really kissed?"

She answered "No! No I haven't."

Her usually smooth skin became bumpy and chilled. It felt like goosebumps going down her spine. Just a few moments ago, she was thinking about how handsome he was and now, she was pretty sure she was about to be kissed by him.

"Come with me," he said, standing up and taking her by the hand, gently lifting her to her feet. He led her to a nearby closet, they walked in and, at that moment, the whole world could have disappeared and she wouldn't have cared.

She realized she didn't care what was going to happen tomorrow or the next day or the next. She figured she was in love. She didn't really know what love was but she wanted him to love her like a child, a lover and a friend. He looked deep into her eyes and said, "Christina, the very first time I saw you, I thought you were the most beautiful girl I had ever seen."

"Thank you." she said, lowering her head, "Nobody has ever said that to me."

He lifted her head and very gently kissed her. His lips were soft and warm and she didn't want him to stop as he held her tightly in his arms. She felt safe and protected, but she knew soon enough, the reality of the situation would steal away this moment. They gradually and slowly slid down the side of the wall and sat on the floor, holding onto each other. She didn't even know his last name, but it didn't matter. The only thing she could think of was the two of them…together.

The grind of the day overcame them and they both fell asleep. She didn't think they slept long but waking with a jolt she realized she hadn't told her mother where she was.

She said, "I think I'd better go. My family doesn't know where I am and I don't want them to worry."

They peeked out the closet. All was clear. They stood up and tried to leave the comfort of this secret place without looking too guilty. As they did, an older woman saw them and said, "I would hate to tell your mother and father what you two have been up to."

"Do you think we will get into trouble?" She looked at Peter, then at the woman, and said, "I really don't think it matters, just look around."

The woman rolled her eyes and turned away. Peter and Christina were young lovers, and had no shame about how they felt. They were in love and that's all that mattered. It was all they had to hold onto in this awful place.

They spent every moment together over the next few days. Food was scarce and the soldiers only brought a small bit of bread and weak soup for them to fight over. They would lie on the floor, folded into each other's arms, but the lack of food and the cold floor, was taking its toll on them. Especially Peter. Peter was not looking well, and he was coughing a lot.

Finally she asked, "Are you all right?"

He said, "I am fine as long as I have you with me."

"I will always be here. I love you," She said, looking up at him. He looked at her and smiled just as the gunshots rang out. They sounded very close. She held on to Peter as tight as she could.

Her mother came running from the other room and called out, "Christina, Are you alright?"

"Yes I am fine mother, how are you? How is father?"

"He is…fine" she said, with a look in her eyes that did not convince Christina, "Now, get some sleep….. both of you."

"We will, mother."

> "We lose ourselves in the things we love.... We find ourselves there, too."
> ~Kristen Martz~

CHAPTER SEVEN
The Leaving

Things were getting worse even though they had not thought that was possible. The days became a week…then two and the sound of gunfire was becoming more and more frequent. They were getting sicker and weaker. They were also being forced to go out into the sun and walk around and the doors to their homes would be shut. Many of the older men believed it was because there weren't as many guards now and they needed to keep an eye on them….and to search the buildings. There were people selling or trading small bits of candy, bread and cheese.

Christina was sitting with Peter on the curb when her mother brought her father out onto the sidewalk and he sat against the building. Christina looked around in horror. How long had it been since she saw him? Her father looked like he was going to die.

He called to her and said, "Christina, do not let this place get the better of you. Be strong my child, be strong."

She looked at him and replied, "I will father, I will…try."

Hours later they announced the doors would be open, so they could go back inside. Slowly, they all struggled back in. Christina, looking back out in the streets, saw many bodies that were not moving. The arguing was getting worse between those who were still here and still there was nothing to eat. The woman who had argued with her mother about the rice was gone, and so was all of the rice. Everything was gone. There was nothing and today the soldiers had left nothing.

The next morning Christina was looking for Peter, but she couldn't find him. Last night his mother demanded that he stay close to his family and they were one floor above them. Christina's father had not built up enough of his strength but said he was going out to get food. Christina begged him not to go, but he insisted. He had to go. He had pulled the small wad of money out of the toe of his shoe, waved it and said, "I will get some bread and water, so we can eat and drink. What kind of a father would I be, if I couldn't feed my family?"

Christina grabbed on to her father's arm and cried, "No father. I am afraid for you, don't go! If we are going to starve than we will starve together. Please don't go."

He repeated, "I am going and I will be back with food."

The sun had set and father had yet to return. Christina went to her mother and said, "I'm going to find Papa."

"No, Christina, you mustn't."

"But I have to find him."

There was a slam against the door and a woman opened it and screamed. It was Frederick. He was bloody and his clothes were torn, several large purplish marks were swelling up under his eyes. Someone had attempted to cut off his beard. Christina had heard of this, the soldiers would give you food for this. In trying to do this they had also cut his face.

Christina screamed, "Father, Who did this to you?"

Aurelia gathered him in her arms.

He reached into his pockets and said, "They took every last cent I had. Now we have nothing, absolutely nothing."

He started to cry. Aurelia was holding onto him and said, "Now, my darling, don't cry! God will provide. God will surely provide."

A man came up behind her, grabbed her by her hair and yelled, "Don't you ever use that name here again!"

Aurelia turned, freeing herself but leaving strands of her hair in the man's clenched fist. She had a look of shock and horror on her face.

The man repeated firmly, "You do not mention God here again. It is because of him that we are here. Now get out of my way."

He began to turn away, stopped and faced Christina's parents, "And if I ever hear you speak of faith or God again, I swear, I will kill you."

As the man moved down the hall Frederick said in a weak and strained voice, "We have lost everything, will we now lose our faith?"

The three of them sat quietly for a long while then Frederick said, "I was told we are not allowed to eat."

Christina said, "What? What do you mean we are not allowed to eat?"

He said, "I heard, whatever we brought from our home is all we would be getting. They will be moving us again, until then there will be no food."

"But we have been here for such a long time now," Christina said, "I was told they were going bring us food."

A man's voice reached out from the other side of the room, "Are you really that stupid? We are going to the camps soon and we are going to work, and the old and weak people will be killed."

"What!" Christina exclaimed, "What are you talking about? That is not possible. You are wrong."

The man said, "Wake up child. Where have you been? Drowning your mind in that stupid drawing book of yours or too busy kissing that boy?"

The drawing book slipped out of Christina's hand and she started to blush. She looked back at her mother and father. What were they going to do about food? She knew she had to go out and try to find something for them and for Peter to eat. She had heard about the area where the non-Jews would throw fresh white bread over the walls into the ghetto. She was hoping God would show her His grace and she would be able to catch some of that bread.

She left the building quickly ignoring the pleading of her mother who begged her not to go. There was no curfew per se but fear kept most inside after dark. Christina did her best to blend into every shadow she could find, curling up and pretending to be a bush or a rock. Her dark clothing was her friend this night as was the absence of streetlights and a new moon. Then the rain came teaming down, pounding against her skin, as if it was trying to skin her alive.

The last few stragglers hurried inside and the soldiers scurried to find shelter in their trucks. She was drenched to the bone but at last she made her way mostly unseen down the streets. She had been walking for an hour, looking over her shoulder, clinging to the wall very still when a truck passed.

The storm was starting to cease and there was a bitter cold knifing its way into her rain soaked body.

She stopped abruptly as she saw a shape in front of her crumpled in a heap at the mouth of an ally and approached it slowly. It was a woman and she had collapsed. The blanket wrapped around her hid all but a bit of her face and her head, covered in a brightly colored scarf. She looked so calm and peaceful that Christina nearly moved on. Instead she decided she must wake her and see if she could walk to somewhere more comfortable. She shook her gently. Nothing happened, she tried to move her and the woman rolled over onto her back. In her arms was a baby and they were both dead.

Christina stifled a scream and ran. Each step took her farther from this awful truth laying in the alleyway and closer to the unknown.

"Please God, Let it keep raining; or let the shadows fall over me," she whispered.

As if, in immediate answer to her prayer, a loud thunderclap came and sheets of rain came down again, like a waterfall. She took shelter under an awning, sunk to the ground, curling up behind a large ceramic pot that held a long-dead tree next to a door. She had to get food and get back before the sun came up. She remembered the words of Mrs. Kowalski. She believed in her and that was enough to keep her going.

Mrs. Kowalski had told her, "Christina, view life as you see it, but filtered through the eyes of God and he will guide you."

She came out from under the awning determined to go on. She noticed a narrow walkway between two buildings. It was barely wide enough to scoot through. Her hand trailed along the rough of the brick wall as she navigated in the dark, careful not to trip, shuffling her feet along the way. She had no idea where this little causeway would end but for now she was safe, surely no one could see her here. The buildings on either side seemed much too long. She had almost decided to turn back when she walked right into a cinderblock wall. It looked as though it had been hastily built between these two buildings to stop passage between them.

Splatters of concrete had squirted between the blocks and fallen to the ground where they were left in clumps. There was nowhere to go but back.

Christina felt the anger rise up and she kicked savagely at the concrete clumps. The ground made a funny noise on her shoe and she stopped, bent over and touched it. It felt smooth. She brushed away the dirt and found a steel plate. Looking closer she could tell that the dirt below had been dug out. This steel plate covered a hole. A hole she was small enough to fit through.

She looked back in the direction she had come and listened crouching down on the ground on all fours. She lay on her stomach and went into the hole. Christina arched her back and pushed up on the other side. It gave way easily and the plate on the other side shifted and she slid it forward. She waited a long time before sticking her head up above the edge to freedom.

The walls of the building on either side moved toward a street a mere three feet in front of her allowing her to be hidden as she clambered out of the hole. Christina replaced the steel plate and hastily covered it with the dirt and cement she had displaced. As she was about to get to her feet, a strong hand forcefully grabbed her by the back of her collar. She gasped, waiting to be shot, as she was spun around and stood face to face with a man. He didn't look like a soldier. Still, she waited for the fatal blow that would splatter her brains all over the wall. She stared at his face in the darkness but couldn't really make out any details. He let go of her collar and grabbed her by the arm pulling her flat against a small door. With one quick motion he reached behind his back grasping the knob, twisted and pushed it open sweeping Christina into a dark room.

He had not said a word. There was nothing inside, save two large containers. By this time Christina was shivering uncontrollably from fright and also being so cold.

The man put a finger over his lips, "Shhh…"

He stuck his head out the door and looked left, then right. It was as if he didn't want to be seen as well. Then he did something that amazed her. He removed his overcoat and placed it over her shoulders. Christina was filled with confusion. He pointed to a little crate and whispered, "Sit."

She sat down. He squatted down next to her just staring at her in amazement. As Christina eyes adjusted to the dim light she noticed first that he was young, very handsome and had a small scar on the right side of his cheek, and deep blue eyes. He didn't look German at all; he looked English and had a dimple on the left side of his face. He was unlike all the other people she had met since all these began. Who was he? She was still afraid to open her mouth. Maybe it was a trick? Maybe he thought she was someone else?

He stood up, and looked outside again; left then right; then came back inside the room. He was standing, still facing the other way and finally he whispered in a British accent, "Where is your family?"

She replied, "They are in the ghettos. I've come out to get food. We are all hungry."

"Which of the others told you about our little tunnel?" He asked.

"Nobody, sir, I..I…just found it."

"Well," he said, "That's a bit a luck, now innit?" He smiled and Christina giggled.

"C'mon," he said.

She slowly stood, still looking at him. His hand reached down. Her eyes followed it as it wrapped gently around hers, and it was soft and warm. A woman knows when a man is hostile, especially when he holds her hand and he was very tender.

He secured her close to his side. They exited the room and glided slowly and swiftly along the shadowy hall. They were deeper in the building when they came to another door and he pushed it open. Walking in, he closed the door behind them.

The walls were draped with a heavy burlap material. He pulled one of the wall coverings aside, and there was a narrow door. Christina was so confused, but it didn't stop her from asking, "Excuse me. Is there a way I can get some bread for my family?"

"Yes," he said, "Keep following."

She stepped through the doorway without fear. Even though she felt safe with this strange man she knew things could go very badly, very quickly.

They were in a very small room. It was some kind of bunker, clean and organized and it was warm.

He said, "Sit here." He pointed to a maroon colored, cushioned chair and she sat down. He came up next to her and handed her a bowl of cold beans and a slice of bread.

"Eat this now," he said and went back to a closet. Christina devoured the food almost feeling guilty. When she finished the man brought her a satchel saying, "Take this to your family."

She looked up and said, "Thank you so much." She thought she might cry.

"I don't know what to say, who are you, why are you doing this?"

"Not all of us agree we must do nutin', my chaps and I have set up this place for those of you brave enough to use it. You know they will kill you…and maybe us…if you are found out?"

She looked away and when she looked up he was gone and she was alone in the room. She staggered to her feet and found her way back to the door they had entered with the satchel over her shoulder. She felt numb. She couldn't believe her luck. Now she had to make her way back to her family and to Peter.

It was not as easy on the return trip. Out the door, under the little tunnel and down the causeway between the buildings. She had made sure the steel plate was covered with dirt and more than once thought that if she could get back here…it was the road to freedom. But the tunnel was small, the causeway so narrow, she doubted if anyone bigger than her could get out.

She reached the street and froze, there were too many trucks and soldiers milling about. She stood there for several minutes trying to devise a plan but could think of nothing.

A loud commotion arose from down the street, opposite of her route. A group of men were shouting. Yelling at the soldiers. Suddenly all eyes were on them as soldiers, with weapons raised stormed up the street. She bolted from her hiding place and ran. She did not stop until she was at the front of the building she lived. Her mother was in the lobby, frantic.

"Where have you been? I have been so worried about you."

"Here momma." She handed her the satchel. She realized then that she didn't even know what was in it.

Aurelia looked shocked. "Where'd you get this from?"

"I cannot tell you, but where is Peter? I must see him."

"Oh, honey, he is very sick and his mother has taken him upstairs."

"No," she said, then raced up the stairs. She saw his mother and asked, "Is Peter here?"

She said, "Yes he is, but he is a very sick child, maybe tomorrow."

"I must see him. Please can I see him?"

Peter's mother moved aside. Christina saw his frail body lying on the floor. His mother looked at her as if to say, 'I think it's too late, child.'

Christina slowly walked to him. He didn't look like the same boy she had kissed just a few days ago. He looked frail and old.

She kneeled at his side, whispering, "Peter, I have brought you ....food." She touched his arm, and he was so cold.

"Peter, It's me...Christina."

He slowly turned his head and said, "How could I forget you." He turned his head away, "All I need right now is you."

She curled up next to him. She knew whatever was in the satchel was not going to fix him. He had an illness with no medicine. He gently took her by the hand and closed his eyes.

"Christina, when we get out of here, will you marry me?"

She said, "Yes, I will marry you." She wiped the tears from her eyes and added, "You will forever be the love of my life."

He whispered, "And you will be mine."

His mother was standing behind her, sobbing and said through her tears, "They have taken everything from us."

She turned to her, angry and said, "No. They cannot take everything from you or from me."

She turned towards Peter and continued, "They cannot take the love that we have, if only for this short time that we have loved each other. It may as well have been a lifetime, a lifetime of love for me and if I lose my love tonight, than I have loved like I may never love again."

Peter opened his eyes, squeezed her hand and smiled. Then he was gone. She laid her head on his chest sobbing, holding his hands for a long time. She rose to her feet and held his mother in her arms. They both wept than she turned and left the room. As she was walking down something the stairs snapped inside her and she began to sing.

"Humpty Dumpty, sat on the wall, Humpty Dumpty, had a great fall. All the King's horses and all the King's men couldn't put Humpty together again."

She went to her mother without tears in her eyes, her voice cold and hard, "He's gone, momma, Peter is gone."

Aurelia said, "He is in a better place dear."

Christina said, "Then perhaps we should join him. I am not sure I can live without him, mama. I loved him so much. He saved me."

The next weeks seemed too brutal to endure. When Aurelia showed Christina what was in the satchel she decided she would have to make repeated trips to her secret provider. It would be the only way they could survive. Cans of beans, vegetables, chunks of bread and the occasional can of evaporated milk kept them alive. They offered what they could and no one asked from where it had come.

On occasion Christina saw other boys, mostly teenagers, pass her on her mission. They did not make eye contact, nor did they speak. The bulging sweaters or bags told her everything she needed to know.

The bad day came. Guards stormed into the building, ordering them all to go outside. She grabbed onto her mother and father and walked arm in arm down the steps, along the same street they arrived from, carrying everything that they had, no matter how small or insignificant it was. She had her drawing pad, with the picture of Peter, rolled up and stuffed into her pants.

After walking out of the ghetto and to the railroad station, they were forced into trains, cattle trains. The look on everyone's faces were mixed. Some were filled with apprehension, horror, or relief reflecting his or her optimism at being free of this place or their impending doom on what was yet to come. The ride was short, frightening and unpredictable. There had been so much propaganda, rumors and lies that nobody really knew what the truth was. The train came to a halt. They had arrived at another, bigger station.

Christina could see through the cracks of the door, a row of soldiers waiting for them. A loud, screaming, heavyset female soldier boarded the train and started to grab random people. She shoved many off, causing them to fall, some fell head first onto the rocky ground below.

The soldiers on the ground were yelling, "Na lewo, Go left! Na prawo, Go right!

Much later Christina would know 'to the left' was to the gas chambers and 'to the right' meant work, hard labor. She was still standing on the train, witnessing thousands going to the left, going to the right: men, women, children. Her mother and father were among those whom were taken to go to the left as a guard moved her in the opposite direction.

She screamed, "No mother. No."

Her father looked back at her, one more time and his eyes told her, 'goodbye'. Just than an officer came up to a girl, who was fighting back, trying to join her family right next to me. He shot her in the head and Aurelia found her daughter's eyes and simply shook her head 'no'.

Christina nodded her head, 'yes', and tears spilled out of her. This, she thought, is what real fear is. One of the soldiers grabbed the girl, who had been shot, and pulled her roughly across the gravel and threw her body in the ditch next to the tracks. The train doors started to close. Christina was still on the train with what seemed to be mostly younger women. All she could remember was her mother crying. She had read her lips, 'I love you. I love you.' and then the doors were shut and the train started to move. She held onto her drawing book underneath her coat. She didn't know it was going to be like this. She thought they were going to be able to stay together.

She prayed, prayed for her mother and father. She prayed for Peter's mother and she prayed for the young girl, who was shot in the head and now laying in a ditch. It could have been her, she thought.

"There's a long road of suffering ahead of you. But don't lose courage. You've already escaped the gravest danger: selection. So now, muster your strength, and don't lose heart. Have faith in life. Above all else, have faith. Hell is not for eternity. And now, a prayer - or rather, a piece of advice: let there be comradeship among you. We are all brothers, and we are all suffering the same fate. The same smoke floats over all our heads. Help one another. It is the only way to survive."

~Elie Wiesel~

CHAPTER EIGHT

RAVENSBRUCK

Once the train had travelled a ways and Christina had found a small area where she could sit, she tried to talk with one of the women. The woman didn't want to talk. She chose another, an elderly woman, asking, "Do you know where we are going?"
The old woman solemnly said, "We will soon find out."
Christina said, "Do you know where they are taking our relatives?"
No answer.
She asked again, louder, "Do you know where they will be taking our relatives?"
She answered with a sigh, "Child, do you really think you will see them again?"
Christina said, "Of course I do. Won't I?"

The woman looked away and they never spoke again. They were traveling far, through the countryside, through towns and villages that Christina could see through the cracks of the car they were in. She recognized Poznan when they passed through, she had been there before. She knew that they had passed into Germany when they crossed the River Oder and the fear rose up in her. She was no longer in her beloved Poland.
When they approached a large train station, they started to slow down and the train came to a jarring stop, clanking and squealing and hissing. There were rows and rows of soldiers, holding guns. The doors opened and everyone was forced off the train. Some, mostly those near the door, were violently pulled out and thrown to the ground. Christina was quick to avoid this as she leaped out,

landing nimbly on her feet. She was shoved into a line and they were ordered to walk, to march. The stragglers were ordered to run, to keep up with the rest.

Christina was exhausted by the time they reached the camp gates. She had done her best, carrying her own little bag and helping the older women by slinging their meager belongings across her back so they could walk faster. The brick walls of the camp were at least fifteen feet high. The wrought iron gates opening outward, were black with shafts and triangles jutting skyward covered in spikes.

They were herded like cattle into barracks, long squat buildings. Christina stopped counting them when she reached forty. All were almost the length of three train cars. They came to a large building and were made to go inside and take off their clothes. Christina had always been shy, but mostly she was afraid to let them see her drawing pad. She knew they would take it away from her.

The crying and the moaning creeped into her as they all started to strip down, she moved very, very slowly. An officer blew her whistle and said, "Go." The naked women all started to walk.

Christina was still partially dressed and holding on to her pad. She began to walk, undressing as she did, holding the drawing pad beneath her blouse. She moved toward the wall, behind the line, blocking her from view by the guards and saw a small utility or tool box. She reached over quickly and shoved her pad behind it, then quickly got back into the line. 'I'll return later and fetch it', she figured.

After they been given 'uniforms', which looked to Christina like striped pajamas and in her case were much to large. She was walking with the other women and she fell back into a memory. It was Mrs. Kowalski again.

"God will guide you," she said, "to the most beautiful places and he will help you paint the most beautiful paintings. Never let anyone influence you. You have an amazing gift; and your hands are his creation."

She stayed in that memory, a lie, as long as she could. It was a place of freedom. This, she thought, was not reality and she wanted to hold onto whatever piece of that lie she could.

She remembered Mrs. Kowalski up until the day she left the school. They were told she had to leave for personal reasons, and she thought of her, crying in the hallway. She had heard the soldiers took her away, some say she was ill. Soon after that, her school was shut down and it was then that the war really came into her world.

Christina was pulled out of her daydream by a blaring announcement that addressed them in their native Polish that said, "You have stayed in the ghettos for two months, and now you are here. You will have to work, and you will do as you are told."

Her first job, along with two other women, was removing buttons from piles of clothes. Christina guessed that the women must've been mostly in their forties. They were to put the clothing into large caldrons, along with dozens of reading glasses, and shoes. She didn't want to think whom these all belonged to.

Hours crawled by. Her back was hurting so badly and sitting on the floor was taking its toll on her. She couldn't imagine how the others felt. She was young, and her tailbone hurt.

She caught a slight movement out of the corner of her eye and turning slightly, saw a man. This struck her as odd, most everyone here was female, even most of the guards. He was standing in the doorway and staring right at her. Their eyes quickly made contact and she looked down and continued with her duties. Her hands were numb and her back was in so much pain. The man walked over to the female officer who was guarding the room. She saw now, as he came in from the glare of the outside, that he was in a German uniform but of what must have been a very high rank. His boots glistened, he wore a hat with a gold braid and a stunning golden eagle above his brow. His coat was draped casually over his shoulders and he carried a command stick.

He engaged in whispers with the guard, they both looked over at Christina. A cold, like ice, was running through her veins. The officer and the guard quickly stepped outside the door and began to talk.

A crazy thought sprang to life in Christina's mind and it was wrapped in hope.

'Maybe they found my mother and Father. Maybe they are going to tell me where they are.'

She stood up and walked toward the door. The woman next to her said, "Stop! Where are you going?"

Christina whispered, "I think they found my parents."

The woman insisted, "No. Stop! Get back to work !" She looked very frightened.

Christina ignored her. The officer was facing the other way, smoking a cigarette. Christina walked right up to the guard and tapped her shoulder. The German spun around, her eyes were pure anger and she yelled, slapping Christina across the face. Christina howled.

The guard's fists came crashing down and she screamed, "No. No, please."

She blocked the flailing with her arms, enraging the guard. She fell to the ground and tucked her head between her knees. She kicked her and kicked again. She flopped over on her side, pain searing through her as she cried out in the little German she knew, "Es tut mir Leid, I am so sorry. Bitte horen Sie auf, Please stop."

The officer, who was just in the room, spun around and stepped through the doorway. He said something in German, then he turned and left. The guard gave Christina one more violent kick into her ribs, pointed back to her workplace and spat on the ground. She crushed her cigarette under her boot, and went back to her post.

As Christina sat down between two women, one said, "Why did you get up? Didn't you know you could be killed for doing that?"

Christina said, "I thought maybe they found my mother and father."

"Zglupiales?" The woman asked, wondering out loud if Christina was crazy and rolling her eyes, "They would never tell you if they found your mother and father. Do you think this is a game?"

Christina said, "Of course, I know it is not a game. I've seen people die. I just want to know if my parents are still alive."

The woman looked at her, shook her head sadly and returned to pulling buttons from clothing.

It was late afternoon when the order came, one they would become familiar with, "Back to your barracks, now."

The women walked in single file back, and the guard they came to know as Binz yelled, "Run!"

Run they did, all the way back to the barrack. Christina lay on the wooden planks of her bunk. There was no mattress, but it felt good just to be able to lie down and sleep took her.

The following day, she was ordered to work in the same building but with an entirely different group of women. Christina found this odd and disturbing. Today she would not be pulling buttons off clothing. They were given the task of separating gold teeth from regular teeth. Christina was horrified. She didn't even want to touch them…she could guess where they came from. She felt the bile rise up in her throat and she thought of her parents. What if they're dead? What if they've been murdered?

A soldier came in, grabbed her by the arm forcefully and lifted her up to her feet. She threw up on his boots. The other women looked at her in horror.

Christina was shaking and said, "What is it? What have I done? Please, no!" she resisted, "No, please no."

After a few minutes she walked along with him. It was no use. She was too weak. They walked pass the rows of barracks. She saw two soldiers carrying the body of a young girl.

"Where am I going?" She asked.

The soldier said, "Commandant Schuster wants to see you."

She looked at him, and asked, "Who?"

Christina was placed in the back of a transport vehicle, the doors were closed. The ride was short. Christina imagined they must have circled the little lake facing the camp and arrived somewhere in the village of Ravensbruck itself. After several minutes the door opened and another prisoner was smiling at her offering her a hand to help her down. She couldn't help but notice…he had no teeth. She looked around at the grand residence. It was perhaps the biggest house she had ever seen…and it was yellow!

Several brick steps led to an entry with four gleaming white columns. The only ugly thing she saw was the giant Nazi flag draped from the eaves on the roof. She was led through the huge double wooden doors and into a foyer of marble and plush curtains. She suddenly felt very dirty, without thinking she wiped her grimy hands on the striped dress and oversized blouse of her "uniform". She stood, alone, in the middle of the expansive room. She was shaking.

A strong male voice came from the room on her left. "Come!"

She walked on wobbly legs and stepped through the double doors. The room was beautifully decorated, with a crystal chandelier and the same marble floors. At the center was a large mahogany desk framed by two poles. She recognized the flag of Germany and the Nazi swastika.

She slowly stepped to the center of the room, then stopped. Her first thought was, 'Am I going to be punished or maybe even killed? Maybe the guard who beat her up told him that she did something wrong.'

The voice spoke again, "Come closer."

She jumped, not seeing him, then realized it came from the oversized chair behind the desk that was facing a window. She moved closer. The chair began to turn. She recognized the officer at once as the one who had spoken to the guard in the workplace.

A small dog, a beagle she thought, was sitting in his lap enjoying the stroke of his master's hand. She just stood there, she didn't have a clue what she was supposed to do.

He said, "Come. Come closer!"

She edged her way to the small chair sitting in front of the desk.

"Sit," He said, pointing to a chair. "Don't be afraid!"

She sat down. Behind him was a portrait of Adolf Hitler. He stared at her for a long time and then finally he broke the silence and said; "You are Christina Nava?"

She hadn't heard her full name in such a long time but she answered, "Yes. Yes I am." She was biting her bottom lip and sliding her fingers along the hem of her grey and white shirt.

He said, "You are nervous."

"Yes," she answered.

He said, "Please don't be nervous."

He lit up a cigarette, and blew the smoke away from her face, and then offered her one.

She couldn't believe it. She couldn't believe he was offing her a cigarette. She reached over and took it. Slowly, she pulled it out of the carton and staring back at him said, "Thank you. I have not smoked one of these in a very long time."

She was lying. She had never smoked in her life. She was too young and she had always hated the smell but then, she was not about to tell him that. She held it between her fingertips in front of her face, studying it, like she was some connoisseur. He took amusement in her play-acting, like a little girl, pretending to be an adult. She looked at the intricate writing and said, "The name is Bremaria. I don't believe I have ever smoked one of these."

He stared at her, then leaned over to light it, asking, "You have smoked before?"

She thought he was trying to catch her in a lie, but was too afraid to tell him the truth and said, "Oh yes, I have smoked."

He sat back in his seat and gave her a polite, but fraudulent smile. She took in a puff and started to choke profusely, saying, as she was shaking her head, "Oh yes, I remember. These are very strong."

He sat there watching her, not taking his eyes off of her, then he laughed. He knew she was lying. Christina felt a wave of nausea pass over her. The lack of food, this vile cigarette. She sat upright and managed to say, almost like a proper lady, "I am finished with this. May I put it somewhere?"

He pointed to an ashtray on his desk.

She stood, leaned over and smudged the cigarette out, and then dropped it in the ashtray and sat back in her chair. He was still staring at her, as if he was studying her. She was already feeling very uneasy and this did not help. Not at all. What did he want? She was sure he hadn't brought her here to watch her cough her brains out on one of those horrible cigarettes.

He then said something Christina found very strange that took her totally off guard, "Life is hardly worth living without an obsession. Wouldn't you agree, Christina Nava?"

She thought about what he just said and then answered, "I guess so."

He continued, "Love is about obsession. Isn't it?"

She didn't know what he was talking about, but if she gave the wrong answer, and got him angry, she could be in real trouble. But then she thought of Peter and said, "Yes, I guess I would agree with you."

He continued, "God himself is about obsession, isn't he?"

She felt her heart thump harder in her chest and did not answer.

"What is your obsession Christina?"

"My...," She stopped abruptly. She was going to say 'My art' when something blossomed in her mind.

"May I ask you, sir, how you know my name?"

"I know of your mother, Aurelia, I have seen her art."

She blurted it out before she could stop, "You know of momma? Is she OK, where is she?"

This time he did not answer. Instead he opened the center drawer and pulled out a stack of papers and started to leaf through them. Christina's eyes grew wide as she recognized her drawing pad.

"Perhaps," he said, "this may be your obsession?"

"I, I don't know what you are talking about."

He stood abruptly, stabbing a finger on the stack of papers, and said, "Do not lie to me, girl, you signed some of these!"

He sat back down calmly and watched the flush rise in her neck.

Finally, he said, "Are you acquainted with love, Christina Nava?"

She sat still before him, with a stomach filled with knots. She didn't know why he was asking her these questions. She was afraid to answer him. Was he crazy? Maybe he was drunk.
Neither helped her in knowing what to say. She raised her, hand like a child in a classroom, and said, "Why are you asking me these things, sir?"

He adjusted himself in his chair and smiled softly. She thought this look was...tender? He reached in his desk, replacing the drawings and pulling out a thin book and opened it. It looked like a journal and flipped through the pages, beginning to read, "I can make you...comfortable here Christina Nava. I can...take care of you. All you have to do is trust me and I will make sure you are not harmed." He closed the book and stared at her. She sat there, feeling so incredibly uncomfortable, knowing she could never trust this...man. She wanted to leave this place.

He then said, "I would like you to dine with me."

She almost laughed through her fear. After all of that, and he was asking her to dine with him? It seemed ridiculous. Since she had arrived the women had received only half a loaf of bread each evening and some "gray water soup". They had heard the bread was baked by the prisoners of the men's camp some fifty miles South of them as they had no cooking facilities.

Was he asking her on a date? She almost laughed again. When she saw the seriousness in his face she said, "Me sir? You want me to dine with you?" She realized she couldn't be in the real world.

This was not the real world. This was a world that belongs to the insane, brainwashed men, who are told to destroy families, to hate and kill. Why was she sitting there? Why doesn't she just stand up and ask him to kill her? Does he want me to not hate him?

She felt like she was going to be sick. Christina pulled away from her thoughts and carefully looked around the room, realizing that if she wanted to get out of here alive, she would have to play along with his game. She was almost certain she was being tricked, so she said, "But sir, I am a Jew."

His face was a stone mask as he stared at her, then she spoke again, "Sir I am a Jew, why would you want to dine with me?"

She waited for his answer, but there wasn't one. Is my attraction that powerful to this man? Suddenly, he leaned over his large mahogany desk, his hand came towards her face, his eyes stared into hers and she thought to herself, "He's going to hit me now."

He didn't. She carefully opened her clenched eyes and a more horrible thought leapt in, 'Oh my God! Is he going to kiss me?"

He gently folded her hair behind her right ear. His eyes still focused intensely on hers and then, bringing his hand away, he accidently, but gently touched her cheek. In that small gesture, she felt a sense of humanity in this man, but she was still confused and still repulsed.

She said, "Yes sir, I will dine with you."

"You may return to your barrack, now."

Christina stood up, gently bowed, like she had just parted company with royalty. She still felt sick as the guard Binz drove her back. She was still in total disbelief. This man, who held the spectre of death above everyone wanted her to dine with him? The entire experience was like a dream. No, it was a nightmare.

All that evening she replayed the bizarre meeting she had had with Commandant Klaus Schuster. How he said he would take care of her, how he said he would watch out for her, but she didn't see any special favors now. She thought of what he might be eating tonight as she gnawed at the stale piece of bread carefully dipping it in the soup that looked like dirty water. She had heard it was from potatoes but had never actually seen one floating in the muck.

Just before dark, Chief Guard Binz entered the barracks with the two sister guards Maria and Anna. Behind them, through the open door Christina could see the guard Herta and her ever present guard dog Greif. She instructed the sisters to start choosing prisoners at random and having them gather their clothes and bedding.

Binz scanned the room and her eyes fell on Christina. Binz was coming toward her.

"You…Come!" she yelled at Christina.

They were told they were moving to new living quarters but Christina doubted that very much. The women the other guards had chosen all seemed older, weaker and none were anywhere near as youthful as she was. Something bad was going to happen she was sure. Perhaps Binz did not like her little trip to the commandant's house.

They made them form a line just outside the barracks. Christina could see faces of those left behind pressed against the glass windows curious as to what was happening.

They were indeed taken to new living quarters. It looked like a huge chicken house, but there were no chickens. There were wooden bunks, with two beds apiece instead of three, on either side with hay thrown on the planks. The smell of this place was rank and thick in the back of Christina's throat. Her body ached and some of the older women were starting to cry from the pain and from the cold.

The door swung open and a soldier came in, it was a male and there were very few of those in camp. Christina had a very bad feeling about this. He watched them closely. An older woman reached up her hand and asked for a blanket to put over herself and Christina learned on that day and at that moment that you never ask an officer for anything, ever, not even if a crazy commandant promises that you will be taken care of. Nothing matters, because the officer pulled out a gun and shot the woman in the head just for asking for a blanket.

There was silent hysteria among all of the women, but Christina imagined a wave of relief passed over her with the words attached

'Thank God it wasn't me'. The soldier left without a word and they heard the bolt clang home locking them in until morning.

Some women were throwing up, some passed out and some were praying. As for Christina, the memory of the Commandant started to fade for it seemed to mean nothing. She was still hungry and colder now, and while this barrack was considerably smaller it seemed more spacious with so few inside. The guards, aside from choosing her to come here, had shown her no favors. That was her reality. Being here with old, sick and dying women was her reality. Knowing that her parents were as bad off or worse, dead even. Sleep finally came and she disappeared into dreams.

She was running through and below the Jasper trees on the green hills and found herself resting under the branches of one of those trees, counting the pink and purple blossoms. She felt the cool soft wind that swept over her, bringing with it the fragrance of the earth. She studied the ripple of sunlight as it scratched it's way through the leaves accompanied by the smell of moist green grass. Peter walked up to her looking healthier and more handsome than she ever remembered him. She reached up to run her hands through his soft hair and then, he started to vanish.
She said, "Don't leave me. Take me with you."

She awoke momentarily and sleep drug her back.

She was drawn into another dream, but this time it was with her little sister, Sha Sha. Her real name was Sarah. She had been struggling with what her momma called "bad blood."

She held her close, Sha Sha's arms wrapped around her. They sat in the middle of a bed. She could feel her sister's heart beating against her body and then one arm fell down limp to her side, followed by the other arm and she felt nothing.

'Now what,' she thought looking up to where her God was supposed to be. The God she believed in and prayed to. But there was still nothing.

She looked down at her sister and knew she was gone. She was the first to know. How could she be the first to know something like this? Did God know she was gone? What a stupid thing to think! Of course God knew. Why didn't she feel anything? She had cried her share over stupid romance books. She'd cry at things that didn't warrant true emotions, but here she was, holding her little sister's body in her arms and she felt nothing. How could she have become so cold?

She had to tell mother. Aurelia walked over to her and looked at Sha Sha saying, "She looks so peaceful. Pick her up, dear and put her into her bed, will you?"

She looked at mother, and slowly a single tear made its way down the right side of her cheek.

"Did you hear me dear?"

She couldn't answer her. She just sat there staring at her, hoping she could read her mind. The words scraped out of her, "Sha Sha is gone momma. Why not me momma? Why not me?"

The slap on her hand brought her out of that horrible place into another. She opened her eyes to find she'd been holding the woman who had been sitting next to her. The woman above her said, "Come child, give her to me."

She had died in her lap, but her eyes were still open…staring at Christina. She recoiled and pushed the body from her. She looked around the room. There were seven or eight women sitting back to back. There were other women, dead, overlapping each on the other side of the room. She felt the bile rise in her throat. She helped the woman who had awoken her drag the lifeless form towards the others as the door swung open.

An officer entered the room, screaming at them to get up and stand in line. She was ordered to pick up the woman, who was dead next to her, and stand in line with her. She had heard that if they didn't walk with the dead, they would be shot. She struggled to pick her up, placed her arm over her shoulder and dragged her to the line. She kept sliding off of her. Christina kept jerking her up close, but her head hanging down was pulling her down. She kept pulling, ignoring the awful sounds that were coming from the corpse.

The guards outside were different. They were prisoners too. They were the Jewish police, who had betrayed the rest of us, in order to try and save their own necks by helping the Nazis. They were as mean as the German soldiers, and some were worse. They wanted to show the Nazis that even though they were Jews, it didn't matter. No questions asked.

She thought to herself, 'How can they do this?' She didn't say a word. She knew better.

The smell of death lingered, and chastised her empty stomach. At last, they were told to go back to the barracks. Christina was afraid she would have to bring the dead woman with her but one of the soldiers slapped the back of her legs and said, "Drop her. Drop her."

She let the woman's body slip from her shoulder to slowly fall to the ground. As they entered the room, they didn't speak or make a sound, all they did was just climb into their bunks.

The next morning, they were ordered to sit in a long row of chairs in the next bunker. Again the Jewish police were giving the orders. One of the women in the line of chairs recognized one of the guards as being a Jew she had known before and said, "You are a Jew. How can you betray us?" She spat on the ground.

The woman she accused bent over and tore the yellow Star of David from her clothing. This meant something Christina thought, but she never had a chance to ask…she never saw that prisoner again after that day.

Christina sat, waiting in the middle of the table as two women at each end began shearing off the prisoners hair. They grabbed large handfuls, digging their dull clippers into scalps. Christina saw many had drawn blood. They had almost arrived at her position when she noticed the guard Binz watching her from the door, she was not smiling. As soon as the hair butcher grasped a good sized chunk of Christina's hair, Binz yelled "Stop! The Commandant wants this one presentable."

Christina was relieved but then realized Binz could have stopped it long before she did. She wanted Christina to suffer, thinking she was next. Once everyone's but Christina's hair had been cut they ordered them to strip down. As Christina began to shed her striped clothing she noticed the hateful stares from the other prisoners.

They were walked outside and stood naked. This was like the Appell, the roll call done at 5:00 am every day and again in the evening. This, Christina thought was different. It was mid-afternoon and they were naked. Now they were told to kneel. The fear in her was as cold as the wind that swirled around her bare skin. The ground was stony pebbles. It was so painful, the jagged rocks digging into her kneecaps brought tears quickly and easily to her eyes. They were kept there until almost dark. It was the worst form of torture she had experienced since she'd been there.

Christina had a wild idea, hoping her commandant would come around and save her, but she knew that wasn't going to happen.

After the first two hours the guards had come and sprayed them down with water hoses like they were farm animals. She guessed that was exactly what they were to them. They threw disinfectant powder on them that made their skin itch and burn. After the third or fourth hour, Christina had lost all track of time.

She was so tired and sore she barely remembered going back into the barracks and flopping down on her bunk. Drifting off immediately, she was escorted into another one of her memories.

She was in school and there was a boy. His name was Jimmy John. He used to chase her on her way to school, but she always seemed to get away from him, until the bad day. He grabbed her and threw her to the ground, then he got on top of her and kissed her on the lips, and all over her face.

Christina had screamed, "No, No. Stop it. Stop it."

She screamed for help while all the other children were laughing but he wouldn't stop. With both of her hands pinned, she was helpless. He was too strong, but she finally managed to get one of her hands free and she slapped him hard across the face, shoving him off of her.

Her eyes flew open and she was back on her bunk. Her dream, it seemed, had not stopped. When she focused, a face loomed over her. For a moment it was Jimmy John, then it slid away into the face of one of the male guards. She had been struggling with the officer, who was on top of her. He stood up and started to unzip his trousers. Panic swept through her, 'He was going to rape me in front of all the others, and then probably kill me for fun,' she thought.

She closed her eyes tight, waiting for the inevitable, hoping that if she didn't resist he may not shoot her in the head. There was the sound of a commotion and she heard heavy boots approaching.

The soldier, who was assaulting her quickly stopped and zipped up his trousers. It was the commandant, who had summoned her to his quarters. He and the officer exchanged words with each other, which she didn't understand. He slapped the soldier, who had assaulted her, hard, just the way she had slapped Jimmy in her dream.

Christina was trembling when Commandant Schuster looked down and said, "Are you all right?"

She set her jaw, looked him in the eye and answered, "Yes. Yes I am."

Schuster turned and looked at the other officers and guards who had managed to find their way in the door, his voice was filled with grit and ice.

"These things will NOT happen as long as I am Commandant, there are far worse things than being a prison guard for women."

He turned to Binz and explained to her that Christina was to be cleaned up and in the morning be brought to his residence to work there alongside the other prisoners taking care of his home, then he left.

Before the Appell, she was taken through the camp to the front gate. It surprised her to see that the truck waiting for her was not being driven by Binz, or any other guard. It was a male prisoner, probably from Sachsenhausen Camp, where they baked the bread. He wore the same cotton striped uniform of a prisoner but also had a chauffeur's hat cocked jauntily on his head.

To Christina's delight she learned that he was Polish and that in addition to speaking her native language he was also fluent in German. The ride took a bit longer than the first time so she was able to learn much from the man. His name was Marechek. He had been the Mayor of his town and a lawyer.

The Commandant used some of the prisoners whom he could trust and had special skills to offer. He asked Christina what her special skill was and she told him she didn't know and she was afraid to find out. That made him laugh. They stopped outside of the residence she had first been summoned to and he opened the car door for her.

Marechek said, "Sie sind ein gluckliches Madchen!"

She looked at him puzzled. He slapped his head and repeated, in Polish this time.

"You are a lucky girl."

She moved slowly through the big doors at the front entrance and was surprised when she saw no one in the foyer, no guards, no prisoners. She didn't know what else to do so she went back to the only room she had been in, the one with the mahogany desk. Commandant Schuster was sitting behind it.

"Come in child, sit and we will talk."

"Have I done something wrong, Herr Commandant? That soldier…I was sleeping, I didn't…" she stammered.

"No, I understand what happened. You are here because I want you to paint."

She looked at him, and he could tell she was confused. He lifted his hand and gestured toward the wall to her right. At first she thought she was just looking at a blank white wall. As her eyes explored it she realized it was not a wall, not at all. It was the biggest canvas she had ever seen.

"That? She asked, "you want me to paint on that?"

"Yes," he said, "I want you to paint a mural. I want to see the beauty of Poland. I want to see what your eyes see: the beauty of this country, the people and the hills and your beloved Jasper trees if you wish and the sympathy of your land."

She was dumbfounded. She thought to herself, 'He speaks like a poet, a poet hiding inside a monster.'

She was not in the Camp and she was determined to do anything to stay out of it. It held only suffering and death. Yes, she would play this game…as long as she could get away with it.

He said, "This will be my office for the time being, but Reichsfuhrer Himmler will be taking residence. Do you know who he is?"

Christina shook her head, no.

"He is, next to Hitler, the most powerful man in Nazi Germany. It is my job to prepare this place for him and I want him to see the beauty of what you paint."

She asked, "Does this man appreciate the arts?"

He answered, "Yes he does."

She thought to herself, 'How could he understand about beauty? He kills and starves people to death. What could he possibly understand about beauty?

She stared at the canvas, thinking of what she would paint. Certainly not what she sees. Death and sadness and immense suffering. She would have to pull from her memories which were quickly fading with each wretched day. Days filled mostly with fear.

Her thoughts turned to the commandant. 'When he's in his bed at night, with a full stomach and a glass of liquor, what does he really understand and what does he expect me, a young woman, who has lost her family and witnessed death at the hands of his subordinates, to paint?'

He looked at her and said, "Well?" He was waiting for a response.

She said, "All right." She turned, looked at him in the eyes and said, "But why me?"

He said, "You are from Poland, yes?"

"Yes."

"And your Mother was a very good Polish artist? Yes?" He asked, continuing without a response, "I want to see if you are as good as your mother."

Christina said, "I will never be as good as my mother, but I am sure you could get the best artists in all of Germany."

He said, "But I want you to do it, Fraulein."

There was that look again. She had no choice.

She stood to her full height and said, "I will, but I need paint. A lot of paint. As many colors as you can. And brushes and mineral spirits."

He said, "I will have the desk and furniture moved and your supplies delivered tomorrow while I am in Berlin.

"Berlin?" she asked, "who will watch me?"

"Do you need watching Christina?"

There was a long silence and then he said, "When you awake you will go to the cook and have him make you breakfast, his name is Jauque. He will find Marechek and he will be responsible for you. Do you understand what I mean by 'be responsible'?"

She knew very well. He was looking at her again, in the tender way he had that first day.

In that moment, she realized how much power she had. This man, Nazi or not, had an infatuation for her and with that infatuation, comes power. She was young, but she knew the power women have over men, and maybe she could use that power...if it didn't get her killed first.

He said, "So you will not disappoint me?"

She said "No I will not disappoint you. Sir, may I have some bread?"

"We can do better than that Christina, tonight you shall eat well and sleep in a real bed."

"Thank you."

He said, "Now go."

A lady with a white apron met her at the door with a tray of food and took her to a small room with a small bed and table next to it. Christina devoured the food. She wasn't even sure what it was....and she didn't care. She fell soundly asleep.

The next morning when she woke she slipped out of the bed and reached for her clothes. Her striped cotton uniform was gone. In its place was a dull pair of gray slacks and a bright blue blouse. She would have made a bet that blue was the commandants favorite color.

She quickly dressed and made her way downstairs to the kitchen stopping by the bathroom on the ground floor. She spent a long time cleaning up, letting the fragrant soup bubbles caress her. She stepped carefully into the kitchen. A very tall, thin man was standing with his back to her. He was dressed all in white and had a funny white hat on. He looked over his shoulder and said, "Ah good, you are up, breakfast is ready...sit down."

Christina walked over to the table sitting in the middle of the room and her face fell and her heart hurt. Sitting on the table was a small piece of bread and a bowl of something ugly and gray. She almost cried. She certainly did not know what to expect but she was sure it wouldn't be this.

"I don't think I am hungry, sir," she said in a weak voice.

The cook, Jacque spun around, put a fist on each hip and scowled, "Why you ungrateful....pffft. Do you know how long it took to prepare your meal?"

Christina looked at the table and couldn't imagine it took very long at all. The cook saw her gaze and laughed.

"Oh missy. No!...haha...that is the food for the dog.

He reached behind him and pulled a plate to his front and placed it on the table next to a fork, spoon, knife and napkin. He was rewarded with a very large smile from Christina as she sat in front of more food than she had seen in weeks. As she stabbed at the ham and large portions of eggs disappeared into her mouth she mumbled, "What…is…this?"

Jacque looked over her shoulder where she was pointing at the irregular shaped yellowish-gray balls on her plate sitting in a puddle of butter and next to a scoop of some red jam.

"Kroppkaka's," he said.

Christina looked up at him with a bewildered face.

"I learned them in Sweden. They are….um…potato dumplings with a bit of bacon inside. The jam you see there are Lingonberrie's, you swirl it into the butter."

Before he had even finished explaining she had attacked the unsuspecting balls and two were gone. Jacque laughed again.

Christina was slurping down the last of her milk when an officer came into the kitchen and said, "Christina Nava...come."

He was a stout man, with a belly that stuck out from too much German beer. She stood and he took her by the arm and led her to the office where she was just the day before. Nobody was there. He turned the light on and said, "There is your paint."

She sat on the ground, sorting the paint by color.

There were five brushes of different shapes and sizes.

The officer turned to leave, walking over to the door. He stopped, looked at the empty desk then locked the door. He took out a flask from his coat pocket. Christina caught the smell of liquor. He took a hard swallow, walked back over to where Christina sat and asked, "Are you Schuster's whore?"

She didn't answer him.

He repeated, "Are you Schuster's whore? Answer me, when I speak to you, Jew!"

He kicked one of the containers of paint, then slapped her on top of the head.

She lowered her head and said, "No, I am an artist."

He said, "You are just a damn Jew. A damn Jew whore."

Still she said nothing, gripping the brushes as her knuckles turned white.

He asked, "What are you going to paint?"

She said, "I have already discussed it with Commandant Schuster."

He said, "But I want to know as well. I want to know now."

He bent down, pinching her cheeks. "Tell me, Jew. Tell me what you're going to paint, whore."

She said, "You must ask the commandant, it is his choice to tell you. I am sure you will see it when it is done."

He grabbed her head and nearly slammed her face into the floor.

She screamed, "No. Stop. Please. Please. No."

To her astonishment he did stop. She lay there, trembling, "Please sir. Schuster will be angry if I am too weak to paint."

He immediately grew angrier, grabbing her hair and stretching her head back so far that she couldn't breathe and then he put his hand on her breast.

She said, "Please, you have to leave so I can start the mural."

He kneeled down face to face with her and said in a low voice, "Schuster is a very lucky man to have a woman like you. You are beautiful."

She scooted back to get away from him and said, "I am nobody's woman."

He said, "Well, you are going to be mine right now."

Christina started to panic. The doorknob of the office jiggled and she heard Marechek's voice.

"Christina, are you all right? You should not lock this door, please open it."

The large German spit on her then said, "Get up Jew. Get up and paint!" He snapped the lock open, shoved Marechek aside and stormed out of the house.

She knew if she didn't start the painting on the wall Schuster would want to know why. She had been ready to, had been looking forward to it all this time. The anger and rage flowed upward. She knew she could not paint the Jasper trees or blue skies, not now.

She looked around…needing release. She brushed against the canvas and it swayed. Looking up she saw it was attached nearly to the top of the wall with hooks but the bottom hung freely. Christina grasped the corner of the canvas and pulled. It came forward, away from the wall. She could actually get behind it! She knew then what she could do, what she must do.

She went to the kitchen and asked Marechek to come into the foyer.

"I need your help, she said, "I am going to lock the door and you will warn me if Commandant Schuster returns, I am not to be disturbed until I say…I…uh…want to surprise him with what I have done."

Marechek had what Christina thought might be a bit of fear on his face but he agreed. She turned on her heel and returned to the room, closing and locking the door. She rolled the big chair from behind the desk over to the canvas, lifted it and set it so it was away from the wall. She could easily get behind it.

She began to paint, not on the canvas but on the wall behind it. She began to paint from her anger and rage. A power came over her as she stroked the brush across the wall, heavy strokes an aggressive motion of the brush. The sky was a dark orange with black and white smoke that bellowed from the chimneys of Ravensbruck Camp. The chimneys were ominous and frightening. They looked like monsters looming up to the sky, she painted the innocents, people in striped clothing gazing upward. She knew that later she would paint the hands of God, reaching down, taking their spirits as they joined Him.

For now, that would do, she had spent her fury and was ready to start on the canvas. The painting, hidden on the wall, would be her testament, her rebellion, her sacrifice and perhaps…her penance.

Hours later, in total exhaustion, she lay on the floor, waiting for Schuster to come. What would he say if he found the "other" painting? What would he do to her? She couldn't even imagine. She needed to get back to her room. She looked at the painting on the canvas, studying what she had done. She could have done twice as much if she hadn't spent her time on the wall behind it. It was beautiful, unlike anything here. The one behind it was ugly but it held the truth. Maybe someday the world would see it so they would never forget.

The door opened and she saw him and was glad she had unlocked the door when she started the canvas painting and told Marechek he did not have to warn her of Schuster's approach.

She saw his silhouette against the waning sunlight from outside. He just stood there. He didn't come all the way in. She was sitting on the floor, waiting, wondering what he was going to do to.

He walked in and silently stood there staring at the painting. She could see his breathing getting heavier. He reached out his hand to her. Grasping it, she rose to her feet, the questioning look on her face reached out in kind to him.

"It is everything I hoped it would be, you must finish it."

He did not release her hand, instead he walked her out the door and led her upstairs. Schuster left her at the door of the bathroom.

"Enjoy your bath," he said, "come to me when you have finished."

Later, she stood in the doorway of his bedroom clothed in the gray pants and blue blouse. She didn't have pajamas. He was lounging on the bed reading a newspaper, sipping on a drink in a large glass goblet.

"Would you like to hear news of the war?" He asked.

"No."

"Then shut the door and come sit with me and we can talk," he said.

Christina felt an odd emotion as she closed the door and sat on the end of the bed. This is not right. He tried to make "small talk" but she felt something was wrong here.

"Perhaps you would like to sleep in a bigger bed tonight?" He asked.

"No, I am fine in the room you have given me and grateful for it."

"I am sure you are grateful," he said, "let's see if you can stay that way. Take off your clothes."

"The best way out...is always 'through'."
~Robert Frost~

CHAPTER NINE

Back To Camp

A few weeks after 'that night', the night Schuster had taken her against her will but had nonetheless shown tenderness and mercy, Christina was lying in the bunk and she was not feeling well. She was afraid. Her breasts hurt and she had been sure her menstrual period should have started by now.

She heard a voice from the other end of the room of sleeping women whispering, "Christina, Christina Nava."

She looked around, but couldn't see anyone.

She heard the voice say again, "Over here." It was a woman looking into the barracks from what should have been a locked door.

"Come quick, she said, "Hurry, follow me."

"Who are you?" Christina said.

"Never mind. Just come." They ran quickly and she kept repeating, "Hurry."

They worried their way between the bunkers and entered a building Christina had never been in before.

Christina asked again, "Who are you?"

"I am Ingrid, Ingrid Schultz. I'm a nurse." She said, "I tend to the others that need help. You are one of his favorites....of Schuster's, aren't you?"

"Yes," Christina said, "I guess so."

"You work at the residence. We see you go every day. Your hair is still long and pretty."

She brought her into another room, and said, "Please lay on the table. How long has it been since your last menstrual period?"

"It's been a long time, I don't know."

She looked at Ingrid; she seemed to be very compassionate and concerned.

"Where does it hurt?"

Christina said, "My breasts are tender and swollen and sometimes tingly."

Ingrid asked, "May I feel?

"Yes."

"My hands may be a bit cold."

"That's okay." she said.

As she was examining her, Christina could sense her tenderness. Her hands weren't cold at all, they were warm and she enjoyed the caring touch. When she was pressing on her; it felt like she was being kissed, not examined. She felt compelled to make conversation, to take away the shyness of the situation and said, "My mother was a famous artist."

Ingrid stopped and said, "Wait a minute. Was your mother Aurelia Navaman?"

"Yes. That was my mother."

"I knew her in the ghetto. I have one of her paintings."

Christina said, "You own one of my mother's paintings? Which one?"

"I have the one with hills that are covered in snow. Every time I look at it, it makes me feel safe." Ingrid placed her hand over her mouth and said, "Christina. Was she killed?"

"I...I...don't know and perhaps I don't want to know. We were separated at the train yard. They were taken somewhere else," she said.

Ingrid continued to work in silence. When she finished she adjusted Christina clothes and took a step back.

"Christina. Can you imagine all the great people that have died since this began, people who could've changed the world?"

"I know," Christina said, looking down, "God touched my mother's paintings."

"Yes," Ingrid said smiling pensively, "And I intend to get more of them once this war is over. Your mother was a very beautiful woman, very beautiful, just like you Christina."

"Thank you."

Ingrid said, "I must continue my examination."

She placed her hands on her and said, "You are so thin. If your breasts are that tender, I need to give you an internal."

"You don't think I'm...," Christina said, her voice trailing off.

"I don't know, I have to check. Please remove your undergarments and put this sheet over you. I will be back in a moment."

She left the room and Christina removed her clothing. When Ingrid returned she had blocks of wood nailed together. They reminded Christina of the little steps at the shoe store where she had placed her feet when trying on new shoes.

"Scoot down," Ingrid said.

She moved her butt to the bottom of the examination table and Ingrid put her feet up on the braces. She closed her eyes as Ingrid spread her legs further apart, very gently.

Christina asked, "Are you a Jew?"

"No I am German."

"Why are you caring for me?"

"My husband was a doctor," she said. "I have been a nurse most of my life. It doesn't matter who you are or what you are if you need care." She paused, and then asked, "When did you last have intercourse?"

Christina thought of Peter….then she thought of Schuster.

"I don't know. It's been a few weeks."

She felt inside of her. Christina grimaced and shifted on the table.

"I am so sorry," Ingrid said. "Just relax, I am trying to be gentle. Please forgive me."

She finished the procedure, took off her gloves, and said, "Sit up please." She had a somber look on her face.

"What?" Christina asked, "Is everything all right?"

"Christina," Ingrid said, "you are pregnant."

"What!"

Christina grabbed her stomach, "Are you sure? I cannot be pregnant. Not here. Not now. This cannot be."

"The baby is very small right now," Ingrid replied, "Would you like me to take it, to stop this?"

"No," she answered with a look of anguish on her face, "There's too much death here. I cannot do that." She caressed her stomach gently, "If my baby is to die. It will die with me."

"It will be alright," Ingrid said.

"I can't have a baby here in this place. They will kill it."

"No, Christina…we have new orders. They stopped the abortions and the starving of the babies. It is said that Himmler himself gave the order after meeting with the commandant. Schuster said there were just too many.

"Then maybe we have a chance," Christina said, "maybe the Allies will come and save us or …maybe…maybe we can even escape."

She looked at Ingrid hard, hoping she had not said too much. Ingrid walked over to the door and for a moment thought she was going to call out to the guard. She listened and then opened it very slightly and looked both left and right to make sure there wasn't anyone nearby, because she was about to help a Jew.

She shut the door, leaned against it and said, "What I'm about to tell you would get both you and me condemned to death, so I know you won't say anything. Christina, I have gotten many to freedom."

"You have?" Christina's heart leapt in her chest, "How?"

Ingrid continued, "Since we have been here, I have been able to get fourteen women and seventeen children to the Orphan Train."

Christina said it slowly, "The Orphan Train?"

"I cannot go into a lot of detail, but I can help you."

"But," Christina said, "the Nazi's must know. How do you account for the ones that are gone?"

A sneer crossed the nurse's face as she said, "The Nazi's don't count the dead."

Christina said, "How do I know you are not setting a trap for me?"

Ingrid said,"You don't. I can only tell you this, being a nurse here in the camps is horrible but I am still a nurse. I am doing what has always filled my heart. I do not offer this to you lightly. If you told anyone 'Ingrid told me she could help me escape', that would mean the death for the both of us. I think we are pretty much indebted to each other. Don't you think?"

"Yes, I suppose so."

Ingrid then said, "Now Christina, I want you to be very careful in what you do if you are positive you want to keep this child."

"Yes I want to keep the child." she interrupted, "But I want the child to escape from this madness, this place. So he…or she, can be one good thing that has come from the horror of this camp.

My mother used to tell me that the artist's hand is a gift from God and that it is God's truest expression and maybe my child could become an artist like me and my mother before me,"

Ingrid said, "Please, you must be on guard. Your father and mother would want you to care for yourself and your child and since you belong to Schuster, take advantage of that. Let me ask you? Is this his baby inside you."

"Yes."

"Is he in love with you?"

"If he knows what love is, then I think he may be." she said, "He brought me into his home and asked me to dine with him and he knew I was an artist and he wanted me to paint a pretty picture in his office that would soon belong to Himmler and that's where he…he…made me.."

It had all spilled out in a gush and Christina sat there sobbing.

"What did you paint?" Ingrid asked.

"I painted the truth and hid it behind a lie and I didn't care if he found it, I didn't care if he was going to kill me or not. My mother and father are gone and a boy I loved named Peter died while we were in the Ghettos, so I just didn't care."

Ingrid said, "Christina, now you have something to care about and I don't want you to work in hard labor or you will surely lose the baby, you are too weak. You must continue to paint your lie, but do it slowly. You must keep yourself free from sex. He must not find out that it is his child you bear. If he finds out, he will take your child and you will never see him or her again. You must keep yourself well. Eat as much food as you can while you are there. After all, it is not just you…alone…anymore."

Several months went by and Christina could still manage to not look pregnant in the oversized striped pajamas. She was sure Schuster knew even though he had not even hinted at it. He had been very busy and there were several days at a time that she didn't even see him. She was driven to the residence, she painted, ate and went back to the barracks. The other women avoided her or gave her a hard time. Christina knew they were jealous…and afraid, like she was a spy for Schuster.

There were a handful she could call friends including Markey. She was a Gypsy, a Romanian. Her people had been gathered up when the Nazi's had spread their special kind of hate along with the Communists, prostitutes, homosexuals, and criminals.

They had met in those first days, working side by side pulling buttons and sorting teeth. After that the German manufacturer Siemans & Halske came into the Ravensbruck Camp looking for slave labor. Rudolf Bingel, the Siemans member of Himmler's friends would render service to Himmler.

Markey was chosen for this task, along with as many as 200 other women who met their criteria. They must be young with good eyesight and pass certain tests. The Meister (foreman) would use pliers to see if the prisoner could bend wire. The Meister would call out an entire block of women and make them hold out their hands. They were looking for those young and agile and checked their hands to make sure they did not tremble. They looked for smooth dry skin and lean straight fingers. Markey had all the attributes and was chosen. It didn't matter that she was scrawny and had a big nose. It didn't hurt that she was beautiful even if they had shorn her of her curly auburn hair. They would march, all 200 hundred of them, out of the camp gates each morning, turning left towards Siemans hill. At lunch they were marched back to camp for their soup, before leaving again and returning at the end of the day.

Markey had told Christina, "I am like you…a good job. No more pulling and pushing carts like a horse. A bright, clean factory with rows of shining clean tables where we wind the copper around spools. The guards are not from here, not Nazi's. They do not beat us.

Christina asked, "Is this what you imagined your life would be?"

Markey could not answer. Among those who had earned Christina's trust and friendship were Loulou Le Porz, the French doctor of Block 10, a British SOE agent named Violette Szabo and another nurse, the Norwegian Sylvia Salvesen. Christina would count these among her allies and protectors. She also had some acquaintance of two of the Ravensbruck Rabbits which were also secret letter writers. The 'rabbits' were prisoners who were subjected to horrific medical experiments.

Christina hadn't felt a lot of movement from the life that grew inside of her. Markey kept telling her she didn't look well, but she insisted, "We all look sick, don't we?"

She agreed with her. She confided in her and told her she was carrying Schuster's child.

The days went by swiftly. Christina, Jacque and Marechek had found some very clever ways to get food and odds and ends back to the camp. Christina was amazed at what could be smuggled in her long hair.

It was Fall when Christina went into labor prematurely. She stumbled through the rows of bunkers, hiding, keeping low. She went to the infirmary, seeking out Ingrid. Shaking with pain, she knew she was going to have the baby. She saw movement and pulled back into the shadows, waiting to see who it was. It was Ingrid.

"Ingrid, it's time. Please help me." She fell to the ground.

As Ingrid prepared her she said, "Please tell Markey."

"Can we trust her?" Ingrid asked.

"Yes, hurry."

Ingrid sent Sylvia who had just arrived to a barrack. She shook the frail looking girl, "Markey, wake up. Christina's giving birth. Hurry, hurry. We are in the infirmary. You must help me move her to barrack C. "

Barrack C was their version of a 'safe house', most of the guards would not enter for fear of getting sick.

"The soldiers are between rounds and will not be coming this way, at least not right now, but we must hurry."

Ingrid and Markey carried Christina to the barrack and laid her on one of the wooden beds.

Ingrid said, "Get me a blanket and sheets from the closet below the sink. Quickly, we haven't much time."

When Markey returned she was sent off again to get hot water.

"Quickly," Ingrid said, "Her water has broken", then to Sylvia

"Yes, this baby is on its way. Put the blanket over her shoulders."

Christina moaned, in her quiet despair. Some of the other women rushed into the room, Markey turned and announced, "Christina is giving Birth."

Ingrid said, "If you can't help, then please leave, I need room and I need light," her tone changed as she was soaking up the water and blood, she whispered, "too much blood, there's too much blood."

Christina yelped "Oh God. God. Please help me."

Sylvia said, "Shouldn't she be in the clinic?"

Ingrid turned, looking at her and said, "Heavens no, if she gives birth in the clinic….we must try to keep this one under wraps. This one will be hidden from Schuster. Then Christina will be…," she stopped abruptly when Christina squeezed her arm, very hard, "then Christina will not be able to go to the residence to paint."

It was a lie, but a good one.

Christina was pushing hard when she felt her body go into spasms. Markey wrapped her arms around her, staying close.

Ingrid shouted, "Somebody bring more clean sheets quickly. Go to the other closet."

Another woman came back with more sheets, "Move away. Let me through."

The baby's crown was in view and a new life was coming into the world. It was a wonderful moment, but at the same time it was also horrible. Ingrid guided the head out as Christina groaned, and she announced, "It's a boy. It's a boy."

Christina said, "A boy, and I shall name him David. My baby David."

Suddenly Christina screamed, "Oh my God. Ingrid, something is wrong. What is happening?" She was still in so much pain, "Something is wrong, Ingrid, help me. I'm still pushing."

Ingrid, was panicking, "Don't push." She checked for the placenta, and then said, "Oh dear God, Christina. You're having twins. There is another baby."

Markey looked at her with kind eyes, stroking her cheek, and rubbing her head. "You're having twins, mama. You're having twins."

With one last push, Ingrid announced, "Another boy."

Christina was crying, "Two babies. Two babies. This one I will name Daniel, my baby boy Daniel."

The woman known as Hanna entered the room and said, "I heard all the commotion, "Christina has had her baby?"

Markey turned to her and said, "She's had twins."

"Twins." exclaimed Hanna, "Are they alive?"

Ingrid looked at her and snapped, "Yes of course, they are alive! It's a bloody miracle." She cleaned the babies as quickly as she could and placed them on Christina's chest, and they immediately began to nurse and after a few minutes said, "We must get you set up in the linen closet, if Schuster asks for you we will tell him you are sick."

"Schuster is in Berlin, we have some time."

Three days after the birth Schuster returned. Ingrid came back to the bunker to tell Christina.

"I think he expects you to go to him tomorrow, he is not happy that no painting has been done while he was gone, I have spoken to Marechek."

Christina said, "They have been very quiet. The others have agreed to take turns caring for them. I shall go tomorrow."

Ingrid said, "That is good. The soldiers have been busy. I believe they are roaming like wolves around Block 24."

Christina asked, "What is block 24?"

Ingrid said, "It is the whore house. Something is going on. I think the train has brought women from Berlin, but they have been there for days. I am sure many of them will be coming to the infirmary for alcohol sickness."

Ingrid had been supplying Christina with rations of bread, and evaporated milk from Jacque the cook but Christina would need more than that if she was to follow through with her plans

"Are they all right?" Ingrid asked.

"Yes, they are wonderful."

"Good, because, Christina, you must leave soon and the three of you must be strong."

That evening Ingrid came to Christina with a woman she did not recognize. Fear bubbled up.

"Christina, this is Anna Solzer from Colgne."

Christina thought this Anna was beautiful and she realized she had make up on.

"You are German, are you a Jew?"

The woman threw back her head and laughed like a man, "No silly girl, I am a prostitute…with other skills."

Anna pulled a small black pouch from under her striped uniform and Christina caught a glimpse of a pretty floral dress hidden beneath it. She pulled out a device and Christina had no idea what it could be. It had a long cord and came with a vial of inky black liquid. Christina felt the fear return as she asked, "What…what is that?"

Ingrid said, "It's a tattoo gun. Anna has been putting the numbers on the prisoner's arms for the Nazi's....hmmmph, among other things."

Christina's eyes went wide and she stammered, "No, not on my babies!"

"Not numbers, child, it's for if you ever get separated. Now, what word would you have them carry?"

Christina said the word,"wolnosc, it means freedom, put the word freedom on their ankles."

Anna then began the process, arranging letter after letter, to spell the word freedom. The babies started to cry.

Christina said, Stop! Does it hurt them?"

"See for yourself," Anna said and gently placed the tip of the device on the back of Christina's hand and made a small dot.

Christina thought it was uncomfortable, like a hot pen writing on her but it surely didn't really hurt. She shook her head indicating Anna could continue.

Minutes later she looked down and there it was, a legacy of the future, the word freedom. Now it was up to Christina to assure them of that.

Marechek was waiting for her when she arrived at the gate. She had a slight limp as she walked and slowly eased into the seat.

Marechek said nothing but glanced at her often on the way to the commandants residence. Schuster was waiting for her in the room where she was to paint. He eyed her warily.

"You look thin, Christina."

"I have been ill."

"Put on your pretty clothes today, won't you?"

"No, thank you Herr Commandant."

"Why is that?"

"I intend on finishing today, sir, and wish not to get paint on them."

"Very well, but today I would like to watch you paint."

Christina set about gathering her paints and brushes, thankful she had completed the beautiful monstrosity that lie behind this painting weeks ago. She began. She worked feverishly, swatches of color bursting from the ends of her hands as she put the final touches on Jasper trees, bushes and clouds.

Schuster watched her amazed and then said, "If you had worked this quickly before you would have had time to finish two paintings."

A flash of fear gripped her. Did he know? No, he couldn't...she was still alive.

Schuster was nowhere to be found when she had finished, it was nearly dark as she arrived back at the camp. She knew this would most likely be the last time she would see him, the house, her painting and hopefully this dreaded place.

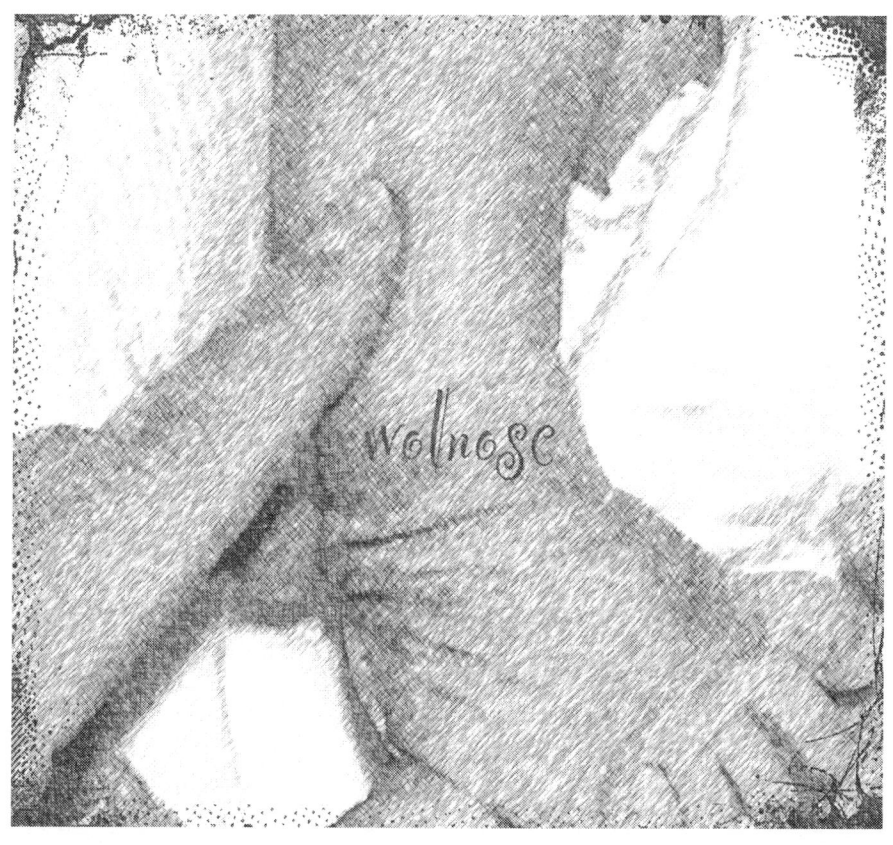

> "For to be free is not merely to cast off one's chains, but to live in a way that respects and enhances the freedom of others."
>
> ~Nelson Mandela~

CHAPTER TEN

Escape

When she was back at her bunk and the guard that had brought her left, they came out of the shadows. It was Ingrid, Markey, Loulou and the British agent Violette. Violette held her two sons, David and Daniel, wrapped in a blanket.

"Are you ready, child? Ingrid asked.

"I have been waiting six and a half months for this moment to come, so I could get my babies to freedom. Yes, I am ready."

"Come, come!" Ingrid said, "Keep low." She followed close behind her then stopped.

"Where is Markey, she is not coming?"

"No, she will fill your bunk to buy us time."

"But I didn't get to even say goodbye!"

"She is the next to go, next time." Violette said.

They moved quickly and soon were at the far North corner of the camp where the soldiers rarely go. Christina pulled down the tiny blanket that carried their precious cargo and uncovered her babies' heads. They were fine. Ingrid assured her that there was a ten-minute interval between the searchlights and the patrol of the Nazis.

"Come on," she said as they ascended a small grade, and reached the fence. Violette, trained by the British Special Operations Executive aiding resistance members in all occupied territories, turned and said, "Shhh, someone's coming."

Christina was sure, whoever it was, could hear the hard beating of her heart. They sunk low, pressed themselves to the ground. She held her babies close to her body, hoping they wouldn't make a sound. Violette had to estimate how much time they had between the guards and the return of the searchlights. They listened intently, listening to the step, step, step…. The footsteps passed by, then faded into the distance and all collectively let out their breath as

Viloette whispered to Christina, "Once we are at the base of that small hill, it is then that we will be at the mercy of your God."

She looked at her and added, "This is the time, Christina, to pray. Pray that God will protect you."

She did.

She looked behind her and then whispered, "Ingrid, whatever happens tonight, I want to thank you for what you have sacrificed for my babies, and me."

"You are welcome Christina, surely I would have been damned if I had not."

We waited and she said, "The light will be coming our way."

She put her hand on Christina's head, pushing her down. She could smell the earth beneath her face as they held their breath. She could see the lights reflecting over the top of them. No one moved a muscle, and then Violette said, "Come, come on now."

They ran, as though the Devil himself was at their heels, making their way up and over the mound where the fence was.

There was a place, where the earth had shifted from the rain, making it easy for a body to shimmy underneath it once Violette had cleared the brush.

Once underneath, it would be their chance to get out of sight, at least for the time being, but they had to get far enough away to free themselves from the searchlights, so they wouldn't be seen as shadows in the distance. They were out of the confines of the camp with a chance for freedom.

They had to navigate their way toward a large body of water that was surrounding the outer region of where they had to be.

Once they did that they were a half-mile from the water, they would be near the coal mine, and it would be there that they could hide. They would wait and at the proper time they would find their way through the narrow gap to the other side of the hill.

Christina checked her babies. She lowered the thin piece of woolen blanket exposing their tiny heads, David and Daniel, her two miracles were asleep. Under the circumstances of how they were born, they shouldn't be alive, and after what she had done she shouldn't be alive either. For the first time Christina believed there was a plan for their lives.

They walked as fast as they could through the muddy and rugged path to rendezvous with the Polish resistance. It would be there that the vehicle would pick them up, transporting them to the train. Having the babies strapped to her chest was making every step more grueling and strenuous for Christina. She looked up to the sky, muttering the words, "Please keep us safe and please give me the strength to do what I must."

They stopped at the opening of the narrow gap they had travelled through. After a few minutes, Violette announced again, "Time to go."

Christina looked up at her and said, "Please, just a few minutes more."

"No." she said, "The longer we wait, the better chance to miss your ride."

Christina rose and continued to walk. She looked at this place, the feeling was somber and a deep reflection of memories brought tears to her eyes. The light from the moon was the only light they had. Over rocks and ruts in the road, she prayed. The air was freezing cold and it felt like her sinuses were on fire. She felt a warm sensation on her top lip. She rubbed her nose, and brought her hand away to a crimson streak of blood. She used her sleeve to soak up the reservoir draining down her face into the right hand corner of my mouth and she kept thinking, 'Keep moving. Keep moving.'

Christina looked up to the moon, like she had done so many times before. She used to watch the moon as a child. It was beautiful to her, and she remembered her mother saying, "Christina, if you look at the moon very carefully you might be able to see the face of God."

She would stare up at it, and she swore she could…but that was when she was a child.

She didn't see the moon that way now, especially being out here. It looked sinister and malevolent, like eyes ready and waiting to reveal their whereabouts and expose them to the Nazis.

She started to pray again, even though she swore she would never pray again in her life, because of what God had put them through. She almost allowed the bitterness to swallow her up much like it had her father, but she wouldn't let it. Not tonight. Tonight she had more important things to do. She remembers her father's words after the soldiers took them, saying, "Pray to a God that allows this kind of cruelty? I have no time for that God anymore."

At the time she thought that was so harsh coming from her father, who was a compassionate man that loved and feared God.

Things change you. She can also remember sitting on her bunk with Markey. She liked talking about her family. She felt it was important to share her stories about her family. It made them feel like they were still human. Markey had such a beautiful vulnerable spirit, and even though her parents were atheists she would sometimes catch her praying at night. Things change you.

Whenever she saw her face in her mind, she saw such love and kindness. 'How could I leave her there?'

Being in a place like Ravensbruck made them all feel the humanity they had in them slipping away, they didn't know what day would be their last. There was so much death around them.

They forged ahead, knowing every minute counted. At that moment Christina's legs gave out and she fell to her knees, landing on her face in the muddy ground.

Ingrid gasped and grabbed her arm, saying, "Get up! Get up!"

She gasped for deep air, holding tight to her children and could hear a faint squeal from one of them. She got herself back up to her knees and thought, 'Would it not be better to take my last breath here in the mud, a free woman than to have to return to the Nazi hellhole, where people end up in a pile of bones, forgotten, or where burned flesh floats in the sky like black snowflakes..exactly as she had painted that vision on the commandants wall?'

She realized she had to get up and slowly stood. She started to cry, "Ingrid, I don't know if I can make it. I just don't know. I am so tired."

Ingrid took her by the shoulders and said, "Christina, we have come this far. There is no turning back, not now. You have to get your mind in a better place. Back at the camps, we will all be condemned. Even though I am a nurse, it makes no difference. We are but animals to them, even Schuster. We will be executed along with everyone else. I plan on getting on that train with you."

"You're leaving too?" Christina said, surprised.

"Yes. I'm leaving too. They killed my husband and my child. Do you think I will not leave the hell of the camps? I have lost everything." Ingrid said, starting to cry, "I have done all I am capable of…now. I cannot return."

Christina said, "I am so sorry Ingrid. I didn't know you lost a child."

She said, "Of course you didn't know. I never told you, but I am telling you now. We shall not lose yours."

Christina, "Okay, let's go."

Ingrid smiled and said, "Violette, lead the way."

It wasn't long until she announced again, "We are almost there."

The words echoed in Christina's mind. Something was tearing at her, making her doubt. She couldn't quite grasp it.

"Christina, they are coming now!"

Christina stopped, turned to Ingrid and asked, "Ingrid, is he here?"

Ingrid looked at her and said, "What are you talking about? Is who here?"

As tears started to trickle down Christina's she said quietly, "God!"

"Yes, he is here Christina."

"Then why doesn't he tell me what I should do?" She seemed frantic.

Ingrid reached out, placing her hands warmly on her face, looking deep into her eyes and answered, "Maybe he already told you Christina. Maybe you just weren't listening."

Christina said, "I just don't know anymore, Ingrid. I just don't know. What if we don't make it? What if my babies die? What if…"

Ingrid interrupted her and said, "I don't want to hear anymore 'What if's'. 'What if's' will only lead you nowhere. It will just blind you from the truth. Christina, whether you go with your babies or had stayed back at the Camps you are going to have to trust somebody, and I suggest you start with your heart, and trust me. I will take care of you, I promise."

Ingrid stared, dead into her eyes, with as much conviction as she could convey, "How do you think I have been able to get so many to freedom, if belief and trust were not a part of our journey?"

It seemed to Christina that a veil was lifted and she saw the truth of Ingrid's words. She had to believe this entire journey was for her sons. They didn't belong in this place.

Christina sat down on an old tree stump, looking into the distance. There was a thick orchard of tall Birch Trees that surrounded the village. Ingrid walked over to her and watched as she nervously kneaded the blanket that her babies were wrapped in.

Christina said, "I think every tree is placed here to keep the main road hidden. Don't you think?"

Ingrid looked at her and then replied, "I believe you are right."

"I feel my babie's shallow breaths against my skin. It's keeping me warm."

Ingrid got up and sat on a wall closer the road. Christina was watching the stars in the sky, waiting for an answer, or a sign, but there was nothing. She looked up and asked, "With all of this beauty and wonder, why can't you tell me what I should do? Why can't you give me a sign?"

She thought about what Ingrid said. 'Maybe she is right; maybe I just don't listen, then she said out loud, "Poland, you are like a baby at the breast of its mother with no milk to feed it. You are starving, just like the people in the camps."

Suddenly, she could hear a very faint humming sound and looked over at Ingrid. She could tell by the look in her eyes; they were coming. Ingrid mouthed, "It is here. Come on. Let's go."

There, in the distance, was the tiniest twin pin lights and the monster that had been hiding inside of her for the entire journey, finally announced itself. The decision, that she had to make, was now upon her. Her heart filled her chest, because she knew it would soon be time to say goodbye….to either her babies, or sacrifice her friends. The Nazi's may not count the dead but Schuster would know she was gone.

The brakes screeched, as the vehicle was brought to an abrupt halt. A tall woman, heavyset and stern, stepped out. Her black hair, streaked in silver, was pulled back into a tight matronly bun and she approached Ingrid, introducing herself as Rachel Carter and said, "I have picked up some others from Sachenhausen, we have water and some food, but only enough for a few, some of you will have to wait, but there will be more water when we get to the train."

"That's fine." Ingrid said, then turning to Christina she said, "Christina Nava is the one, who will join us."

Without waiting for an answer the woman asked, "And these are the babies that you will be taking? How old are they?" Her words were sharp and direct.

Christina answered, "Newly born, ma'am."

Rachel slowly pulled the blanket down, exposing their heads, then placed it back, pursing her lips and sternly asked, "Are you their mother?"

Her eyes of interrogation followed her up and down intimidating her. Christina stood tall and said, "Yes. Yes, I am their mother, but I am not going."

The woman's eyes snapped towards Ingrid, "The mother is not going?"

Ingrid was stunned, she turned and said, "Christina, what are you saying?"

"I have to go back, when Schuster learns I am gone he will kill everyone who befriended me, Markey and all the rest. I must help the others." She felt a bolt of reality tear through her.

"No ma'am. I am not going."

Ingrid stood there slack-jawed, eyes wide. Christina's words echoed inside of her head. She had made her decision.

The woman asked, "And what would inspire you to make such a foolish decision?"

Ingrid, not hesitating, said, "Come with us? Please?"

"No," Christina said. "Please, don't make it harder for me. Just go."

Ingrid said, "Okay, if you want to be like that. If you don't go, I don't go. What is wrong with you?"

"Schuster," she said, "Schuster is what is wrong with me. He is insane, and if I am not there, he will take it out on Markey, Hanna and Sylvia."

Ingrid said, "Why do you want to die, like all the others and how do you know if those women will live if you return?"

"I know they won't die tomorrow." she answered, "I will not be the reason and Markey…is pregnant. How can I turn my back on her?"

Ingrid said, "Oh Dear God."

She became suddenly quiet and then said, "Christina, I love you too much to allow you to die in the camps."

She came up to her, "Christina, you are such a gifted artist; nobody cares about your art in the camp and I know you love Markey, but she would understand."

Christina snapped, "Understand? Understand what? That I left her behind, when I told her I'd be with her until the end?"

"You told her that you were escaping? Why would you do that? How do you know she is not going to say something?"

"She promised." Christina said, "like I promised you. We were supposed to get on the train together. I cannot leave her. I love her, Ingrid. I love her like my baby sister, like Sha-Sha."

"Your goodness will be the death of you, child."

"I've been told that," she admitted, "and I hope not."

Ingrid gently pushed her hair in the back of my ear.

Christina looked up, and said, "My mother used to do that."

"And what do you think your mother would want you to do?" Ingrid asked, "Wouldn't she want you to come with us?"

"I know what my mother would want me to do." Christina said, putting her head she began to cry, "Go Ingrid. Go in the car, just go."

Ingrid held on to her softly pulling her arm away from her, "Stop it. Please stop. Just go." Still making no eye contact, Christina said, "I will survive, I promise."

The nurse shouted, "Get in the vehicle! Be with your babies."

Ingrid whispered to the woman, "No, It's no use."

"We have to leave now." The woman demanded, "Give me the children. We are on a serious deadline. We must get to the train's destination before daylight. There will be another vehicle coming in three months, maybe by then this horrible war will be over."

Violette came out of the shadows and said, "No, give me your boys, I will go with them if you trust me."

Ingrid started to protest but Violette said, "The woman is right, the end of the war is coming, the allies and the Red Army will free you soon if you live that long, I can do no more here, at least your boys have a chance." She looked at Christina and there was compassion in her eyes.

She wrapped her arms around Christina then slowly wrapped them around her babies and said sadly, "I wish you could have brought me all of the babies, but I know that would be impossible."

Christina handed her the bag of bottles, "They will need to eat in an hour's time. They have been such good boys."

She paused, letting it all sink in, then added urgently, "Where will they be going?"

Violette said, "Switzerland, they will be going to Switzerland."

Ingrid turned to the woman, and said, "Go. Just go."

The woman shook her head, got on the truck and just like that… they were gone.

The truck faded away into the distance and all Christina could see in the distance was shadows and the silhouettes of the mountain range against the fading headlamps.

She felt cold inside and sat on the ground, staring into the distance, numb and dead inside. She missed her mother, father, Peter and now Daniel and David. Her neck was still warm from her babies breath. Had she made a mistake? She knew in her heart she had done the right thing, but what was the cost? Her life….Ingrids?

If it had not been for her, Ingrid would've been on that train. She looked up to the sky, looking at the stars through her tears. Prisms of light, colors flashing before her eyes and she said, "Why didn't you stop me? Why didn't you force me into the car?"

She pounded the ground in anger, horrified by her actions. She pleaded with the sky and the universe. She had been taught to have faith but where had that gotten her now? She didn't know. 'Will they be safe? How will I know?'

"I am sorry Ingrid, I am so sorry."

Ingrid came up next to her, placed her arm over her shoulder. Christina turned to her and grabbed her as hard as she could, holding tightly onto her coat and cried, "What did I do? What did I do, Ingrid? "

She was sobbing so hard, she could hardly breathe.

"Why didn't I go with you? What is wrong with me?"

Ingrid stayed quiet, and then she said, "Christina sometimes women suffer terrible, emotional problems after giving birth. Some women even kill their babies."

Christina pushed her away. Nothing else needed to be said.

Walking back to the camps with Ingrid, she thought, 'I will always dream of my babies and hope they will feel the sun on their faces and the beauty of life. Maybe once this war is over, and if Poland ever returns to what it used to be, with her snow covered hills and the pink and purple flowers of the Jasper Trees, and maybe if I escape with the others, I will see them again. There were too many maybes. So she prayed they would remain together, or if separated, find each other through the artist's hand. All she could do now was try to survive, to help the others. Maybe Violette was right and the Allies were coming, she hoped they would find her alive.

Somehow, she ended up lying on her wooden bunk back in the barracks. She couldn't remember how.

She was stiff and sore. How long had she been laying here? She didn't know. As she crawled from bed, the events of the night before weighed on her. Had she really given up her children?

She found her way to the front of the camp where Marechek was waiting to take her to the commandant.

All she could think to paint was the hand of God coming down and picking up every innocent person who had not committed one crime and the wrath of God unleashing his mighty power on the cruelty and malice of these monsters, but she would paint the truth, because that's what her mother always told her, to paint what she saw. She didn't care if he killed her. He will have to look at the horror face to face.

She stepped into the room that held her secret. The huge canvas that held the beautiful painting had been tossed in the corner. The painting that held the truth…her truth, was exposed.

She was alone in the room. Her first thought was to run …anywhere.

Schuster appeared in the door. He walked in and looked down at Christina. His face was a mask.

"What is this? What did you do?"

Christina said, "I painted what I see."

He said, "I told you to paint the beauty of Poland…this is what I get? I asked for beauty and you have betrayed me." Tell me Christina, what would happen if Himmler saw this?"

He didn't wait for an answer. His rage consumed him. His boot lashed out and kicked her. She screamed out in pain. He grabbed her by the hair, drug her across the floor and began smearing paint across her face.

"I would show this to him…and let him deal with you as he wishes….but I allowed this to happen in my home. I let my feelings for you…change…affect me. I have no compulsion to hasten my own demise. Get out, go back to the camp where you belong. I will deal with you later."

Christina had changed since Schuster had returned her to camp. The forced hard labor she had been assigned to was wearing her down. Eating, like the others now, she was rapidly losing weight and getting weaker every day. Her hearing had become acute and her senses had become heightened. She noticed much more now.

This morning it was quiet, too quiet, an eerie sort of calm hung over the camp. She was used to hearing moaning and the occasional crying, but now there was only silence. She knew one reason was that there were many less prisoners now. The showers of gas and the crematoriums worked around the clock. The stench of smoke was everywhere.

Last night, after another endless day digging the sand, she had been stopped at her barracks door by the woman known to her as Yvonne, another British agent like Violette.

"Come child," she said, "you will be sleeping in my barracks tonight. We have a big day tomorrow."

Christina had been so tired she hadn't even asked why. Now, as she awoke, she realized she was alone in the barracks. 'Where were the other women?'

She uttered a small "Hello?" Is there anyone here?"

The door began to open and fear told her they had finally come for her, to follow the others to a fiery death. Again she was greeted by the face of Yvonne. Her eyes were steel and her frown was etched across her face.

"It is time, you must come now!"

"No," Christina pleaded, "I can't, please hide me, I must be able to see my boys again!"

Yvonne grabbed her by the arm and yanked hard and said, "Don't be a fool. Many have died so that you may live. The white buses are here, the Swedish will take you from the camp now. We must hurry, the Red Army, the Russians are coming and Schuster is looking for you…COME!"

Yvonne put a blanket over Christina's head like a shawl and they ran into the chaos forming in the courtyard that had been used for roll call.

Her mind went to Markey and Ingrid and she panicked, calling out, "Markey, Markey, Are you here? Are you here Markey?" She didn't get an answer. There was too much noise and confusion.

Yvonne kept shoving her toward a line of white buses just outside the gates where prisoners were clamoring to climb aboard.

"Where are the others?" Christina wanted answers from Yvonne, she needed to know her friends were safe.

"I do not know what happened to them but Schuster has taken them from the barracks when he was searching for you."

Christina resisted as Yvonne tried to get her into the bus.

"No,' Christina said, "we must find them first."

Yvonne said, "I am sorry, there is no time. Not if you want to see your boys again."

Christina was jostled to the back of the bus, where a lone empty seat awaited her.

Her eyes desperately searched for either of her friends and found nothing. She sat down craning her neck to see around the women and out the window.

"Do you know where the nurse Ingrid is and if you saw a woman with her?" she asked the prisoner next to her.

The woman quickly shook her head, no. Tears were streaming down her face. The woman placed her hands over her face and Christina turned away.

As the bus began to lurch forward, Christina was astonished to see how many were being left behind.

"If they survive a little while longer, even an hour or two, more buses will come, after that the Russians will free them."

Christina turned to see who had spoken. It was a nurse, in white, that Christina figured must be one of the Swedes. She threw questions at her rapidly. From her she learned the Himmler had ordered Schuster to increase the exterminations because those that were still alive would have to be evacuated and all records destroyed, burnt with the bodies. She settled back into her seat, the blanket still around her head and shoulders. She was about to remove it when she saw him. Schuster was outside the gates with several armed Nazi's. One had a woman by the hair walking her forward. It was Ingrid. Schuster was still looking for Christina, maybe he would let Ingrid go on the bus if she gave herself up.

Thoughts of her sons filled her mind as she clamored to the front of the bus. As she reached it she heard a collective moan from the other riders and turned to see Ingrid being hoisted by her neck. Her feet kicked and then were still as she swung from one of the speaker poles at the end of the rope. Schuster turned his attention to another prisoner and Christina saw it was Yvonne, her rescuer. He pulled his sidearm from its holster and put a bullet in her forehead. Christina couldn't watch anymore, they were dying for her, for her sons and it too much to bear.

"Oh my dear God no, Oh my dear God no. No, no this cannot be." She wept.

The driver turned in his seat, placing his hand on her shoulder and looked at her with compassion. He didn't need to say a word because his eyes said everything. She rocked back and forth; to minimize the pain she had deep in her heart, thinking if she had left the camp with Daniel and David, Ingrid would still be alive.

The driver spoke, "We are going to relocate you to the American Safe Zone in France. It is not safe where you once lived. There have been a lot of lootings and rapes, many by Russian officers . Forty-one Jews were killed by nonmilitary."

Christina took some time remembering the home they had lived in, a home she would never return to nor wanted to. She could still see her mother's paintings that were hanging on the walls except for the one that her mother had not finished. It was there. In her mind, but it was laying in the street destroyed by bullets. In her mind, she stood there in the doorway. She could see her mother, sitting on the balcony terrace…painting, and she saw her father sitting at his desk, whittling his little wooden sculptures. They both looked so happy. She shook her head back to reality as the bus moved forward.

"Inside each of us, there is the seed of both good and evil. It's a constant struggle as to which one will win. And one cannot exist without the other."

~Eric Burdon~

CHAPTER ELEVEN

Warsaw, Poland 1956

Johnathon Milner arrived at Dr. Sherman's office unannounced. He knocked four times before the doctor answered the door.

"You!" Dr. Sherman said, "I thought I had seen the last of you."

"I must see you….now!" Milner said through gritted teeth.

"I am with another patient, you must make an appointment."

"Now…see me now and I swear I will never bother you again."

"That is very tempting," Sherman said, "but I am with another patient."

"How long?" Johnathon asked.

"At least an hour."

"Then I will wait."

It was over an hour before the doctor would see him. He ushered him in.

"What is this all about?" Dr. Sherman asked.

"I have found her!"

The doctor made them tea and sat quietly waiting for Milner/Schuster to speak.

Johnathon began:

"I knew that a lot of the women prisoners were housed in a village called Targowek Warsaw, so I purchased a home there. I searched for Christina, but nobody seemed to know where she was, or even who she was, or if she even lived in the community."

I got an honest job in the town square as a grocer. I hoped that if Christina lived there, I would be able to find out where she was.

I put notes on post boards asking if anyone knew of an artist by the name of Christina Nava, but got no response. Years had gone by, and I have never given up hope. I believed that I would find her. I worked hard; saved every penny I could, so I could pay for a home that was not tarnished by guilt. You see, after our sessions, I wanted to start over. I would sit under a tree in the back of my property, thinking of her. I had never considered anyone in my life, and now here I was thinking of only her. I promised myself that if I found her I would take care of her for the rest of our lives. One day, while I was bagging groceries for a customer, I overheard a nurse, who was a regular in the store. She was talking to a friend, telling her of an artist, who she had been taking care of at a Red Cross Hospital in Warsaw. She mentioned that the woman was a survivor from the war, and how sad it was that the woman was no longer able to paint. My ears tuned into the conversation and I immediately put down the bags I was just packing for my customer, saying, Please, please excuse me. I will be right back. I walked over to the nurse and said, 'Excuse me ma'am'.

I could hear the storeowner yelling in the background, 'You can't just walk away from your duties.' I turned back and said, 'Please one minute.' I gave a gesture of apology and then said to the nurse, 'Please, ma'am, forgive me. I overheard you talking about a woman who's an artist from the war. Could you please tell me her name?

The nurse, slightly stunned, asked, 'Might I ask who you are?'

" My name is Jonathan, Jonathan Milner. I work here in the store."

The nurse said, 'Yes. I can see that.'

"I am a very old friend of an artist by the name of,"... I choked up. "Christina, Christina Nava, and I know that she was a prisoner in the war."

The nurse paused, and said, 'Yes, yes, I do know her.'

"Doctor, at that moment my world stopped and I feared my heart would follow it.

'Where is she?' I asked.

The nurse looked at me suspiciously and said, 'Well I can't give you that information, but if you leave me a message I will give it to her.'

I was stumbling over my words. I thought to myself, I can't tell her who I really am.

The nurse was looking at me very suspiciously waiting for me to answer.

"I had to think of something, then I said, 'Yes, could you please give her this message?'

'Yes,' said the woman, 'but hurry, I must go. What is the message sir?'

Please tell her. I was choking on my words doctor but managed to say, please tell her that I want her to dine with me.

The nurse looked at me, smiled and repeated, 'You want her to dine with you? Will she know what this is about Sir?'

'Yes, I believe she will. If you can also tell her, that I loved her. The nurse gave a smile, and said, 'yes, of course, I will tell her.'

She turned and left. My heart was ecstatic."

The Doctor leaned back in his chair and said, "So, did you find the woman?"

"No, I still have not found her."

"Did the nurse ever return to the store?"

"I never saw her again."

"How long has it been?"

"It's been weeks and I have been in much distress from what I have been through, so I was relieved of my duties and my heart remains broken. Maybe she was never meant to be mine; at least, not the way I wanted to have her, because I wanted to use her as my healing, but love should never be used. It should only be cherished. I cannot get that from one who is not there but will you forgive me doctor? If you say yes, then you will be the first person, who has ever forgiven me, and if I don't find someone who will, I think I really will go insane."

The doctor walked around his desk, came up behind him, placed his hand on the shoulder of the anguished man said, "I will forgive you Jonathan, but you....you must forgive Klaus. You must forgive the man you were, and I don't want to know what you have done; that remains in the past. I am not here to condemn you or judge you; I just want to help you, but I have to tell you that much of it is up to you. Sometimes forgiving ourselves is the hardest thing to do, but you must, so you can move on with your life."

"Thank you doctor." He got up and left the doctor's office.

Three weeks later Jonathon found the hospital Christina had been at. He also discovered that she had been sent to a hospice facility after it was determined there was no more that could be done for her. She had a slow cancer that would eventually take her life. Until then all that could be done would be to make her as comfortable as possible.

The next day he drew out what little money he had saved and left for Switzerland. It was risky but if he succeeded he would have the blood money he had received from Sieman and the Nazi Party and placed in a Swiss Bank deposit box prior to the end of the war. Enough to buy the little cottage in Tergovik in Christina's beloved Poland. There she could live and be provided with the best care possible. He knew it was a nearly impossible dream…he also knew it was his only chance to redeem himself and rid him of Klaus Schuster.

"I dream my painting, and then I paint my dream."

~Vincent Van Gogh~

CHAPTER TWELVE

Chicago, June 1976

David Anthony Clark is turning 34 today. At least this is the day his American adopted family chose to be his birthday. He was almost two years old when that happened. By the time he was 10 or 12 he knew he was a Camp Baby, that his mother was a concentration camp prisoner during World War 2, but that was all.

He tried when he was younger to locate some record of her, he felt the need to know if she was even alive and had escaped the camp.

Hell, he didn't even know where she had been held. The only time he felt his mother's presence was whenever he picked up his paint brush. He felt a kinetic pull to his heritage. What little his adopted parents knew about his mother was that she had been an artist and it helped her survive the horrors of the camp.

Living in Chicago with his wife of twelve years and his two kids, Andrew and Sarah, seems like a million miles away from the war and anything his mother would have ever known.

When David was little, attending Eli Whitney Elementary School, he was constantly getting in trouble for "doodling" in class when he should have been reading. His abilities as an artist were brought to the attention of his parents after many visits to the Principals office.

His adoptive parents, previous Peace Corp volunteers and refashioned Hippies, decided it would be easier to help their son embrace his art rather trying to stem its steady flow.

A sketching pencil or a paintbrush felt as natural in his hand as a baseball bat or football for his friends. How obsessed and how good he was soon became evident.

His High School Art Teacher came over one evening to discuss with his parents the possibility of enrolling him into the Academy of the Arts. His parents were so proud of him, and said, "yes." He was enrolled the next semester.

There were many competitions and he won nearly every single one. Many found it curious that he had such a fascination with the holocaust. Most were unaware that was perhaps the only thing he knew about his biological mother. He was careful to enter only a few of those paintings.

His teacher called them "beautiful monstrosities".

At 18 years old, he was enrolled into the Chicago University of the Arts and he was to be one of the youngest enrolled. When he showed the university the first in a series of paintings that would assure his admittance, it was of the holocaust. They found it most impressive. They too were curious about his fascination and how detailed and intricate it was. His official bio told them as well, that his mother was, in fact, a prisoner of World War II and that the painting was inspired by a series of recurring dreams.

He explained in an essay. It read: "As I grew up, my dreams intensified and there were always a woman who held on to my hand, screaming for me to run. I could never see the woman's face, but she was crying and the ominous chimney was in the background. We were running together, holding each other's hands, and then we would get separated. I called to her, but I couldn't see her anymore. Suddenly, I knelt down, praying, and next to me was another boy and we were joined together. I looked down and I noticed he too, had a tattoo on his ankle just like I did. It said the word freedom. In Polish. I would wake up in a sweat and this dream went on for years. I don't have the dream so much now, but I felt I had to paint what I saw as a tribute to the Holocaust, and the six million lives lost, especially a tribute to my mother, wherever she is."

He had another different kind of dream, one that builds inside you and doesn't wait for the night. He dreamt of one day getting artwork into the galleries here in Chicago so he enrolled to spread that message. So the world would not forget. David would walk by the different galleries on his way home from the Academy, looking at famous artist's work but developing a vision of his own. His burning desire to paint was borne of his love for color and texture and grew to illicit strong emotional feelings in those that viewed it.

Competitions and small local showings brought the attention of his unique style and his attention to detail.

In his Junior year he was approached by Brian Pilchard, an agent, who had worked with many famous artists, including Sonya Wayland, who painted healing and depression art. It is the kind of art that stimulates the brain with color, especially for people, who struggle with depression. He also represented Craig Lascar, an impressionist, who did abstract body art.

Brian loved David's work and he had a special love for survivors of World War II. He was an active supporter of the Museum of Tolerance in California and knew David's work would fit well in the cadre of artists he represented.

He told David he too had a relative who had died in the war. Unfortunately, he had fought for the wrong side.

One evening David was watching a T.V. talk show, called The Roger Preston Show. The show had various guests on that talked about political as well as some deeper topics. He announced that he had a special guest, who would be joining him on the show next week.

He said, "It's a woman by the name of Denise Defournier, who had actually escaped a death camp during the War. We have heard all about the hideous experimentation the Nazis did on men, women and children. It was a horrible time in our world and we can only hope and pray that this atrocity will never happen again.

Ms. Defournier will tell you in her own words her incredible story, and the compassion she had for the ones who were left behind. Her memoir, published in 1948 called Ravensbruck: The Women's Camp of Death is used worldwide in historical research. Be sure to tune in. It will be a show that you will not want to miss."

As soon as David heard that, he managed to acquire two tickets to the taping, one for him and one for his wife, Catherine.

Catherine said, "Maybe, after the show, you can introduce yourself to her?"

They made sure they had front row seats. The host of the show came out and announced, "As we have promised, here at the network, we have somebody very special that, I think you will find, truly amazing. It is my pleasure to introduce to you one of the bravest woman in the world, a woman, who was able to survive the death camp at Ravensbruck, and is here with us tonight, to share her compelling story. Ladies and gentlemen, please give her a warm welcome, Miss Defournier."

There was loud but respectful applause and David watched as this small framed woman walked slowly onto the stage with the help from one of the television staff. She took her seat and they brought her a glass of water. She was so kind and thanked the man, who had helped her. Her demeanor was pleasant and her eyes, a light blue, with hair, a silvery gray. There wasn't a hint of bitterness in her.

They listened as she began to talk about many women she knew as friends in the camp as well as the killings for no reason and the soldiers that could shoot anyone just for asking a question, with no remorse. As she was talking, David felt a connection with this woman, almost as if she was speaking directly to his heart, something important.

David turned to his wife and said, "I think this woman is talking to me."

Catherine looked at and said, "What do you mean?"

"Something is stirring inside of me. There's a reason I'm here today. Maybe she knew my mother."

Catherine replied, "Sweetie, you don't even know your mother's name? You don't know anything about her."

David could see the sympathy in Catherine's eyes, he could hear the reason in her voice. He had never felt this before. He couldn't take his eyes off of the speaker. She started talking about a few of the women she had known, saying, "There was one woman in particular and she was the bravest woman I had ever known. She would've done anything for anyone, even at the risk of her own death and proved it during her stay. Her name was Christina, Christina Nava and she was a wonderful artist."

David nearly fell off his seat, his heart quickened. He knew in his heart she was talking about his mother. Glancing down, almost in remembrance of the woman she spoke of, she looked up and continued, "And there was another woman, who was able to get many to freedom. I believe she got twenty-three woman and seventeen babies to freedom, but she lost her life just before the end of the war. Her name was Ingrid, Ingrid Schultz. I was one of those women. First we had to get out of the camp to a vehicle and then the vehicle would transport us to the train, the quietest train I have ever heard, called the Orphan Train. They called it that because so many children were rescued that way either causing them to become orphans or preventing them from being the orphans by escaping with their mother.

There were so many who attempted to escape, but when the Nazis discovered that there was an attempt, they would force them into trucks, give them shovels and pick axes, drive them into the forest, order them to dig large holes in the ground, little did they know, they were digging their own graves."

The woman had tears in her eyes and said, "I admired these women, who sacrificed everything for others. I have nothing but love for them."

After the woman left the stage, David went up to her before the crowd approached, and introduced himself. He briefly told her his story and she asked him what camp his mother was at.

David said, "I don't know exactly, but I keep having these dreams about a woman and I think it is my mother. In my dream, I see her painting, but she isn't painting on a canvas, it is a large wall. I don't know why I see a wall, but that's what it is. It is very vivid, then she turns and a man walks in and starts beating her, saying 'Why did you paint this?' The woman is screaming and begging for her life and I wake up."

The woman said, "My boy, this dream doesn't specifically say your mother was a painter. Dreams can be very deceiving."

David said, "I know that but I feel such a deep connection to her and the fact is that I am an artist."

"Well Himmler loved his art," the woman said, "and there were many artists, who were captured by the Germans much like Christina."

She encouraged him to try to find his mother. He thanked her for her incredible story and shook her hand.

She said, "You are welcome, my dear, and good luck. I hope you find her."

She slowly walked away, greeting many others. It was all very emotional.

In the weeks that followed his dreams came back with a vengeance.

He thought, 'What if she knew my mother? What if she is the Christina Nava she spoke of.'

He wasn't able to paint anything. He wasn't able to focus. His wife was worried about him. The galleries needed more of his pieces, but he couldn't give them anything, he was in an emotional downward spiral.

David went to a therapist named Dr. Margaret Wilson, who specialized in people that experienced their creativity being blocked by emotional stress.

She said, "It is very common, I suggest you paint your dream. Get it out of your mind and get it on the canvas. Let the artist inside be free."

David said, "I have tried to paint the exact image I am dreaming, but something is not right."

She said, "David. What I see in you is a very deep, creative thinker. You are not going deep enough. I want you to try Yoga and meditation. Go deeper and let it all come out."

David agreed with her, thanking her for her advice and then said, "I'm going to paint every detail, every single detail. I'm going to keep a drawing pad next to my bed, and the minute I wake up, I will draw exactly what I saw."

That very night, he was tortured with the dream. It was as if it had been waiting for him. The woman in the dream was running and people were screaming. She was reaching in back of her holding onto a child's hand and behind her the chimney scratched at the sky, framed by the soot and black snowflakes that were the prisoners. Then she was at the wall, painting the scene of fire and horror. David sat up in bed, sweating and crying.

No matter how depressed he was, he was determined to paint the dream or the dream was going to ruin him. He reached for his nightstand, picked up the pad and sketch pencil and began to draw. He finished the night with no further dreams and when he woke he went directly to the studio and started the painting: the chimney, the people, the woman, the mysterious wall, the fire and the snowflakes.

He heard his wife coming down to the art studio and watched her face carefully when she looked at what he had created.

Her face betrayed her shock and she said, "No wonder you have been tortured by this dream. I am so sorry honey."

David tossed his brushes aside and looked at her with tears spilling out his eyes.

"So how is this going to help? Will it help me find my mother?"

Catherine hugged him from behind, kissed his neck and said, "I don't know, I don't see how."

David turned to her and said, "Catherine, Do you believe in supernatural powers?"

"Like what?" she asked.

He said, "Like psychics or mind readers?"

"Well, yes, I do to some extent, but some say it's only a show, and it's all fake."

David said, "But what about that woman, who was able to help the police find that little girl a couple of months ago? What if I hire her to help me find my mother? Catherine, I have to find her. I've tried everything."

"Do you think that's wise? I know we can afford her but I don't want her to take advantage of you," she said, trying not to discourage him, "do you think you might be taking this too far?"

David looked at her, set his jaw and said, "This is something I have to do."

His wife, smiled at him and said, "Well then hire a psychic."

David shrugged his shoulders and with a sheepish look on his face said, "There is no harm in trying."

"No." she responded smiling, "There is no harm in trying."

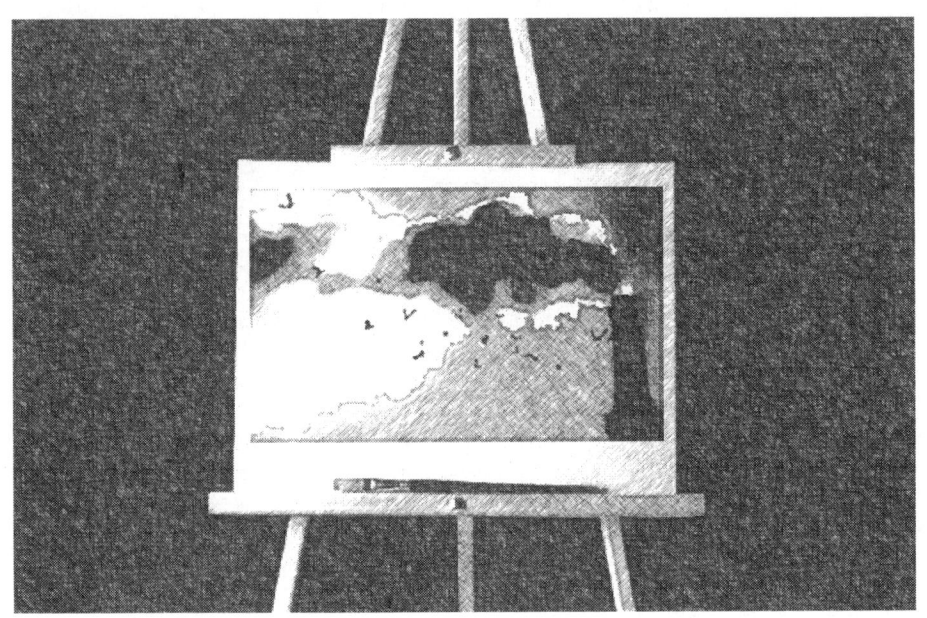

"In the concentration camps, we discovered this whole universe where everyone had his place. The killer came to kill and the victims came to die.

~Elie Wiesel~

CHAPTER THIRTEEN

Warsaw, Poland
April 1957

It was early evening and Jonathan was sitting by the fire in his home. It had been a long day of emotional turmoil as he had been reliving all his visits to Dr. Sherman, his trip to Switzerland and his negotiations on purchasing the little cottage he had found in Tergovik. All of these thoughts left him numb.

He got up and put a kettle on for hot water to make a cup of tea and looked in the refrigerator for something to eat. He remembered a box of tea biscuits he had purchased from the store the day before.

He heard the whistle bellow its loud annoying sound, telling him the water had reached its boiling point. As he walked to put the teabag into the cup there was a knock at the door. He jumped, looked out the window and saw a woman standing in the cold. He opened the door and a small petite woman stood shivering. He quickly and politely invited her in and asked, "Can I help you?"

She answered, blowing warm air into her gloved hands, "No, but I can help you, my name is Monique Stein…might I please have a cup of tea?"

"Oh, yes. I am so sorry. It must be freezing out there."

They both sat and warmed themselves in front of the fire, as she continued, " A friend of mine, who I work with at the nursing home in Warsaw, told me that when she was shopping at Drakov's grocers, she was approached by a man inquiring about a woman who was an artist in Ravensbruck Camp during World War II."

"Yes, that was, that was me." he said, felling a lump growing in his throat. Jonathon swallowed hard and asked, "Do you know where Christina is?"

The woman responded, "Yes I do."

He looked down at the floor and thought, 'Am I really going to find out where she was?'
Jonathan looked at the woman and said, "This is amazing. How is she?"

The woman answered, "She is very ill, and she needs hands on care."

"Ill? How ill is she?"

The woman smiled slightly. Her eyes told him she was not going to divulge too much information; at least not yet and then continued, "With the proper care she may live another 15 years or more. The sickness in her is a bastard…but he is a slow bastard.

The home is running out of funds and she needs better care than we can provide. My friend told me you were once in love with this woman. Do you know if Christina has any family?"

"I… I… I don't know. I don't think she does."
He was afraid this woman was going to pry into who he really was and how he knew her, but finally he answered, "When I knew her, her family had been executed in the war, so I don't think she has anyone at all. But ma'am, I would be willing to care for her."

The woman was quiet and Jonathan thought to himself, 'Oh no! Here comes the question of how I know her.'

He remained quiet.

Finally, she broke the silence and asked, "Are you sure you would you be able to take care of Christina?"

His heartbeat slowed to a normal pace and Jonathan answered, "Oh yes, yes, I will."

At that instant, he began to have a silent conversation with himself in his head. 'Could this be? Will I finally be allowed to take care of my beautiful Christina? Will she rebuke me?'

He looked up and asked, "How did you find me?"

She responded, "It took me some time, but I was able to ask the right person at the store you worked at.

The woman smiled and said, "The nurse by the name of Natalie told me about you and said, 'you seemed like a nice fellow,' and I thought it was really kind that you wanted to dine with her and she accepted your request."

"When will I be able to see her? Please I will do anything."
The woman said, "Soon, but before you do, Christina has asked that all arrangements be made and she be moved before you see her."

"Whatever it takes," Jonathan said, "whatever it takes."

An hour later Monique Stein walked out of Milner's house with all the information she needed to have Christina transported to the cottage, including the keys and quite a bit of money help with the transition.

Jonathan's heart was full but his mind was troubled. After all, the last time he had seen his Christina he had beat her and sent her back to the Camp. He thought about the years that had gone by and how he had changed and how his heart had been softened. He was a new man, but would Christina even give him a chance to prove it ?

Exactly two weeks later Jonathan drove himself to the cottage where Christina had been taken. He was greeted by the same Monique Stein he had met at his house.

Monique told Jonathan, "She has had all her medications and therapy for today. There are instructions and contact numbers on the kitchen counter, I will be back tomorrow."

"Wait," Jonathan said, "aren't you going in with me?"

"No," Christina has insisted she be alone when you arrived."

Then she was gone. Jonathan quietly slipped through the front door, glanced at the papers on the counter and slowly walked down the hall to Christina's room.

The woman lying in the bed was almost unrecognizable to him. She was gaunt and seemed frail. He thought she might be sleeping and lingered in the doorway.

"Come in, Herr Schuster," Christina said.

"My name is Jonathan Milner now."

"You will always be Commandant Klaus Schuster to me."

Jonathan heard the bitterness in her words as he said, "Christina….."

She cut him off saying, "Be quiet….I have some things to say first and you will listen. When my nurse at the hospital came to me with a story of a man who 'wished to dine with me' I knew it was you. At first I was frightened, afraid you would come and then angry that you could. Somehow you had escaped your past and were living in the very country you sought to destroy. Then, when I sent Monique, I was afraid you wouldn't come. I spent many hours and days thinking about whether I would kill you or turn you in to the authorities. When I found out about the cottage I realized I had a third option. I imagine you must have changed. I saw a glimpse of a good man even back in Ravensbruck. I am willing to stay here…with you but there are conditions. You will take care of me until I die. You must know that regardless of how you feel about me…I will never love you. Oh, and one other thing…you will help me find our sons."

"Son's? Jonathan said, "you…we… had twins?"

Jonathan left the room sobbing and Christina did not see him until the next day.

"But are the twin souls destined to be together? Synchronicity is at work here to bring the two back together again. How entrancing to find the same magical alchemy still at work, just as it was at the first meeting....."

~Chimnese Davids~

CHAPTER FOURTEEN

New York, June 1976

David had found the name of the highly recommended medium from a friend on the Chicago PD whose name was Jacqueline Clothington. She had been used in a number of investigations for the police. She wasn't too pricy and he made sure his son was at a friend's house, and his daughter was at a sitter. David and Catherine would do this with no interruptions.

Jacqueline came in, looked around the house and asked, "May I have a tour?"

"Yes," David said, "Of course."

She went through the lounge to the kitchen and then said, "I wanted to get the aura of your home. How old are your children?"

They looked at each other and then Catherine responded, "They are nine and twelve."

Jacqueline sat down and asked, "May I have a cup of tea?"

"Oh yes," Catherine said getting up.

While she was in the kitchen, the woman said, "You are very lucky to have a supportive wife."

She kept looking around the room. Catherine brought the tea service and the woman said, "Thank you dear."

Then she looked at David and asked, "So what brings me here?"

"Shouldn't you be able to tell me?" David joked.

"It doesn't work that way."

She said it with no malice but David could tell she was not amused. She was looking into his eyes as she took a sip of tea.

David cleared his throat and began, "I keep having recurring nightmares and they are ruining my life. I am an artist and I work for the Chicago Institutes of the Arts, but lately I have not been able to paint."

The woman asked, "Are you not able to paint because of the dreams or are you just stuck?"

"It all stems around the dreams and my "mysterious" past," David told her making quote marks in the air around the word mysterious.

"The dreams started when I was a boy."

The woman said, "It's about your mother, isn't it?"

"Yes, it's about my mother. She was a prisoner in a concentration camp."

The woman said, "Oh my. I am so sorry. So tell me your dream?"

David recounted the story he had told more than a few times. Running, chimneys, screaming. He suddenly felt very tired and wondered if all this was just a waste of time and money.

"There is more, yes?" Jacqueline said.

David was visibly startled. He had never told anyone the rest of his dream. He figured this was as good a time as any.

"I am kneeling and praying and there is a boy, who is next to me and we share something but I am not sure what, just some strong bond."

David pulled down his sock, to reveal a small tattoo. It was hard for Jacqueline to read so she asked, "What does it say?"

"I looked it up," David said, "it means 'freedom', written in Polish."

"Where did you get it?" she asked.

"I..uh..I don't know."

Changing the subject David said, "I guess I was hoping you could tell me if my mother is still alive and if so is she here in America or in Poland. That was where she was born, or at least, that is where I think she was born.

The woman looked at him and asked, "May I have your hand?"

He held it out and she took hold, closing her eyes and squeezing the hand. After a moment released it, opened her eyes up and said, "I think your mother IS still alive."

"What else can you tell me?" David asked.

Many things are about to happen in your life, David. There will be an airplane trip, a meeting with strangers and I see a raven. I must warn you, there is a lot of darkness around you and the thoughts of your mother have enslaved you. If you are to be truly free, you must follow this path."

"You're right," he admitted, "But how did she escape?"

She looked at him, and answered, "I don't know. I cannot tell you that for certain. There is a very confusing energy around you, perhaps because of your father? It is like I am being pushed out of it. There are some things I cannot know."

Catherine, still sitting silent squeezed his hand. The woman's eyes were closed, and then they popped open she said, "You have a brother, don't you?"

David said, "No. I am adopted."

The woman continued, like she hadn't heard his answer, and said, "You have a brother! A twin perhaps."

David couldn't believe it and answered, "I don't know." He was beginning to wonder if this lady was a kook.

She said, "These are very strong messages and feelings."

David asked her, "Can my mother send a message if she is dead?"

Jaqueline lowered her head and said, "Oh, yes. The dead send messages, but you just have to be in the spirit to hear them."

"What is the message?" David asked.

She laughed a little and said, "Oh dear, I'm not that good but consider this, no mother would want their son, or sons…to give up.

There is a reason you have that tattoo on your ankle and I suspect your mother put it there. Do not give up your search. You must find the wall. You must find it."

He looked at his wife, then back at the woman, and asked, "The wall? What does that mean?"

The woman said, "I have no idea."

"I painted it." He exclaimed, "Do you feel that she is alive and do you know when I will see these strangers?"

Jacqueline stood up, offered her hand and said, "No, but I hope this has helped. I am happy to have met with you." David shook her hand and she left.

That evening David had been reflecting on the whole experience, mulling the things the psychic had said and letting them knock around in his head. A brother…the wall….a raven. None of it made sense and was disturbing.

He had another nightmare that night, but this time, the lady that had appeared in his dream dragging the child was running away, crying in the middle of nowhere. She was calling out his name, "David, David. Come to me. Find your brother and bring him with you."

He woke in a panic, breathing hard, wondering if he could handle what might come. 'What if she's dead?,' he thought, 'What if I find out that she's been murdered, which is a possibility, and what if I do have a brother.'

He talked to his wife about it. Catherine, ever strong, ever supportive said, "We just have to wait and see. Either way, I'm here for you, babe."

The weeks to follow were better. David had begun painting again, the nightmares had stopped and he had sold quite a few pieces.

The following week his agent told him that he had heard about a sculptor, Daniel Duluth, who was said to be this generations Auguste Rodin. David thought to himself, ' Wow, no pressure there, how do you follow sculptures like "The Thinker", "The Kiss" and "Caryatid Under The stone" ?'

He had never seen Brian so excited and he knew he wanted to recruit more artists and incorporate different types of art into his company in order to expand into Europe.

It was the 1st week of November and he had planned a trip to New York to meet this sculptor. The piece was going to be presented at "Rockefeller Center" and the event would be well attended. He asked David if he would join him. David begged off suggesting his time would be better spent catching up on his own art. It was not until after the flight had left that David had remembered Jacqueline's mention of an airplane.

"If you flee from the things you fear, there's no resolution."

~Chuck Palahniuk~

CHAPTER FIFTEEN
The Coming

Brian studied the people leaving the showroom he was headed for. There were a smattering of 'ooos' and 'aahhhs' as the well-dressed crowd chattered their way to the next exhibit.

Brian passed through the arched doorway that bore a bronze plaque with 'Daniel Duluth' etched on it. He noticed a few small sculptures on pillars and some larger ones, including a man, laying on the ground, his arms reaching up to God, his clothes torn. He looked closely at the detail. This guy, whoever he was, was extraordinary.

He went to the next piece of work, which was of a child, her face was almost grotesque, all skin and bones and the name on the sculpture was, 'Camp Child'. On the wall above the piece was a small white card, words neatly printed on it, the name, "Hanna, survivor of the Holocaust." And a photograph of a woman, in black and white was below, along with her testimony about surviving the death camps.

Brian couldn't believe his luck, to find a sculpter that used the same thematic elements as his best artist. Daniel possessed a passion for the Holocaust just like David.

As he turned the corner, there was another crowd around a larger piece in the middle of the Gallery. Brian gently pushed his way through the crowd and stood before it. The glass of Champagne he was holding slipped through his fingers to the floor, shattering the glass everywhere. People moved away, looking at him and a man asked, "Are you all right sir?"

He muttered, "Yes…no…I am fine. Sorry," his eyes still fixed on the sculpture.

One of the staff, towel in hand approached and also asked, "Sir is everything all right?"

"I am so sorry." Brian said, staring at the piece of art. He couldn't believe what he was looking at and said, "This artist?"

"His name is Daniel...."

Brian interrupted, before the man finished, "Yes I know his name, but where is he?"

The man responded, "He has just finished a tour and will be speaking here in a few moments. He is amazing, isn't he?"

Still in a trance like state, Brian said, "You have no idea."

Brian studied the sculpture more carefully. It was a three dimensional representation of David's latest painting. The one from his dream. The woman, the child and the chimney. It was detailed in what Brian thought must be a thousand shades of gray.

A woman walked up to the front of the sculpture, introducing herself as Muriel Conrad. She was Daniel Duluth's friend and Curator and said, "You will be hearing from the talented Mr. Daniel Duluth momentarily; please take your glasses of champagne and wine, and make your way to the next room. Mr. Duluth will be joining us shortly, thank you."

Brian jostled his way to seat in the front row. The room filled quickly and soon Ms. Conrad stepped to the podium on the stage and announced, "We want to thank you so much for coming tonight. Mr. Duluth is very excited to be able to share with you his work and the amazing story of his life. Ladies and Gentlemen please welcome the talented Daniel Duluth."

There was a tumultuous applause and whistling, as a tall thin man approached the podium and began to speak into the microphone, "Good evening ladies and gentlemen, I am so happy that you have come tonight to hear my story and view my work. First, indulge me as we visit my unusual adolescence. Whittling. This word has gone out of date but it was a passion for me. I started to whittle, every little piece of wood I could get my hands on. I carved my way through puberty. Even my adopted mother's favorite wooden figurine, which I believed sorely needed some alterations." He paused as the crowd laughed, then continued, "You know a young boy's imagination must be stimulated. Well, my mother didn't think so," the crowd chuckled again, "I moved into more serious sculpting with clay and stone when the famous Michael J. Drayton, whom I had admired for years, noticed me. He saw one of my pieces and he graciously agreed to sponsor me. He gave me my first chance to stand up next to the great sculptors and learn from them and told me I had what it took to create 'beautiful monstrosities' and here I am now. Some of you may think that my work is very dark, and it is. Some may think it is too disturbing, and it is. But it is history, our history, we created it and unless handled properly, will only repeat itself, and we, as a nation must be sure that this history is never repeated. You see, my mother and father were prisoners of War World II, and though I have no knowledge of who they are, or if either is still alive, I am deeply moved by that part of history and believe people need to be aware of what happened. I imagined I felt my father's hand guide me as a child as I whittled. Joseph and Mary Duluth adopted me and they were gracious and kind, and gave me the best life a boy could ever want. I'm an only child and we lived here in New York City."

Daniel pauses a moment, glancing at the front row. He spots Brian sitting slack-jawed, eyes wide. He continues, "The piece that occupies the main gallery, my largest, was a very emotional piece for me. It was inspired by a series of nightmares, so I had to take it out of my head, put my hands to work and turn it into something I could feel, touch and remember and the little boy in the corner, I guess, represents myself. As you see, the boy is kneeling down praying to God, with the ominous chimneys of death in the background. It is a metaphor, as if to say God has not taken his eyes off the horror of what happened during those years. As you explore my other pieces of work keep in mind that they are all a tribute…. and a dedication to my father and mother, and all the souls that were taken during that horrible time in our world. I believe our children must be aware of what went on in the world and all we can do is pray that it never happens again. Thank you so much for your continued support and thank you for coming. Enjoy the food and drinks."

The applause was deafening and Daniel left the podium, mobbed by people asking him for autographs and asking questions.

Brian was shaking, he could hardly breathe. He quickly arranged a meeting with Daniel and his agent the day after tomorrow.

Back at his hotel room he called David and said, "David, what are you doing?"

"Talking on the phone," David laughed, "Of course. Everything all right?"

"I don't know....I need you to trust me on this one, David."

"OK, what do I need to do, Brian?"

"Just pack your bags."

"What...wait....why?" David asked.

"No questions, I booked your flight and I'll meet you at the hotel."

David started to object until Brian said, "Either do it or fire me!"

"I have never known you to be like this," David responded, "Are you sure everything is all right?"

"I am fine," Brian answered, "Just pack your fucking bags. You are leaving in the morning."

David said, "What happened in New York?"

Brian said, "David, you are going to be blown away."

David said, "Okay, I needed a little vacation anyway".

David hung up after writing down all the travel details and turned around. Catherine was standing in the doorway with a cup of coffee.

"Did I just hear that you are going to New York in the morning? she asked, "or was I imagining things?"

"No you weren't imagining anything?" David said with a slight giggle, "And yes, Brian was acting very strange. Well, I guess I'm on the next plane tomorrow."

The day flew by and David found himself in back of a cab in front of the hotel, puzzled. Brian had refused to tell him anything. They pulled up to the gallery and got out. David watched the cab pull away.

"Uh, Brian, you know this place is closed, right?" David said.

"We have an appointment." Brian showed the security guard his ID and they were let in.

"This is impressive." David said.

They walked in and Brian said, "This way."

David studied the different sculptures by Daniel Duluth. They were beautiful. He looked at the old man and the child called Hannah, and about her life in the Camps of Ravensbruck, and David turned to Brian and exclaimed, "Holocaust?"

Brian said, "Come on." They turned the corner, where a woman was flipping through some pages There was a large sculpture in the middle of the Gallery. They walked around it toward the front. The first thing David saw were the chimneys followed by the line of people, a woman running dragging a child and a boy kneeling in prayer.

David froze, mesmerized as Brian said, "Now you know why I didn't want to tell you."

David said, "Yes, I now know why. Who is this guy?"

Brian said, "We're going to meet him right now."

Brian walked up to the woman, who was presenting yesterday and told her that they were ready. She scuttled away and Brian turned to David and said, "He is one of the best modern day sculptors I have ever seen."

"But Brian!" David said, he was holding out his hand, his finger stabbing in the air, pointing to the sculpture.

The woman returned, looked at David and said, "Yes, and may I ask who you are?"

Brian introduced him, "Yes, this is David Anthony Milner a very renowned artist from Chicago I am his agent and curator and I wanted him to attend this meeting. He is …um…very interested in Duluth's work."

The woman said, "Yes, wait right here. I will get Mr. Duluth."

Brian looked at David and asked, "Are you all right?"

"Yes, I guess, if you call feeling like I am about to throw up, feeling all right."

The quick click of footsteps preceded him as Mr. Duluth appeared before them.

"My name is Brian Pilchard and I am the agent and sole proprietor of Pilchard and Pilchard in Chicago. This is David Anthony Milner and he is an artist that I represent in the city.

"Yes," said Daniel, "Come over here."

They followed him over to a row of seats by a small table and a waiter came up to them and asked, "Would you like a drink?"

Brian, Daniel and David all said, "Yes, that would be great."

The waiter left and Daniel asked, "How are you enjoying the city?"

David answered, "I have only been here a couple hours."

Daniel said, "So what is this all about?"

Brian said, "You two have something in common."

"What is it?" said Daniel.

"I want you to look at this," Brian said, pulling out a 8 by 12 size photograph of David's painting, it was remarkably similar to Daniel's sculpture.

Daniel studied it and said, "You copied my work?"

"No." said David, "This is my original painting, I am not the one doing the copying."

Daniel said, "What do you mean your original painting?"

David said, "It is a painting of a recurring nightmare that I have had ever since I was a child."

"What?" Daniel exclaimed. "What do you mean?"

David continued, "My mother was a prisoner of World War II."

"If this is some sort of a joke, well it's not funny, I'm calling Security," Daniel was furious.

"No, No," said David, "This is no joke."

Daniel stared at David and something clicked. He calmed down but his eyes were blank when he said, "What do you mean your mother was a prisoner of the War and you've had recurring nightmares?"

David told the story nearly verbatim from his official biography. The silence was long and stretched between them. A very uncomfortable mood rose up it was a mixture of hostility and confusion.

"You know that is also my story? Daniel said.

"I do now." David replied

Daniel said," I need another drink."

David had a crazy notion flash through him. David said, "Look, what do you make of this?" He reached down and lifted up his pant leg of his trousers, pulling down his sock, exposing the ankle that said the word freedom.

Daniel said, "Oh my dear God," as he revealed an identical tattoo of his own, "that means that we are…."

In unison they both said, "Twins."

Hours went by and David had told Daniel about the visit from the psychic. He called Caroline and spent a half hour excitedly telling her what had happened. Before she hung up she told David that the lady from the TV show had called and had wanted to reach him. She had passed along the hotel number. Daniel was still there when the phone rang. A woman introduced herself as Gisela Nachnamen.

David asked, "Who are you looking for?"

She said, "Are you David Clark?"

"Yes, I am."

She said, "I have some valuable information, regarding your mother."

"I have been praying for this call. So what do we have to do?"

The woman said, "We?, Is your brother with you?"

"Yes, but how did you…how could you know? I only found him two hours ago."

"Aw, well fate is fortuitous," she said, "I need the both of you to come to Poland."

"Have you found our mother?" David asked.

The woman said, "Do you remember the name Christina Nava from the TV show with Denise? She says she knows your mother…and she was at Ravensbruck. Just make sure you are both on the flight. I will meet you at the Ravensbruck Memorial and Museum."

David quickly explained to Daniel who wanted to know more.

David said, "I don't know any more. The woman only said that she has something to show us then she will take us to meet the woman who says she knew our mother in the camp."

"Okay. All right, let's go. I hope this will lead to something."

"I know." said David, "Me too."

Two days later, they were on a plane that flew directly into Frankfort airport, where they had to change to another plane that flew to Warsaw Airport. The entire journey from New York to Warsaw was a seventeen-hour journey and as they got off the plane, a tiny woman greeted them at the gate, speaking very broken English but it was easy to understand. She asked, "Did you both have a good flight?"

"Yes we did, a little stiff but it was fine."

She said, "My name is Gisela Nachnamen."

"It is very nice to meet you," said David and Daniel. "So do you have news about our mother?"

Not answering she said, "Please come. Come." She waved us on.

David looked at Daniel and they both walked from the arrival terminal to the baggage claim.

She said, "I have arranged for a car. It should be here in just a moment. Do you have luggage?"

David said, "We both have one small bag."

She said, "Will you please excuse me?"

She walked over to the payphone, spoke for a few minutes and then came back and said, "Follow me."

They exited two large double doors and a black vehicle was waiting for them.

They tried to strike up a conversation with the woman, but she wasn't talking.

She sat very still, clenching onto her purse. She never looked at Daniel or David. She studied their appearance in the reflection of the vehicle window, as they were looking the other way. They both resembled Christina, even though they were fraternal twins, there was something strikingly similar. They were tall, dark and extremely handsome. They were driving through what looked like museums of war buildings and then, they pulled up to large iron gate.

A German voice came over the speaker and she answered back in German. The gates opened. They drove through. It seemed to be one of the concentration camps. They got out of the car, walked across the gravel road and entered an elevator.

The doors opened and once they exited the elevator, they were in the museum. They walked past displays of artifacts, photos and memorabilia.

"What are we doing here?" David asked.

The woman said, "You will see."

They approached rows of memorial tablets, with thousands of names carved on them. Above it, written with the most aesthetic handwriting was The Ravensbruck National Memorial.

As they walked through the door and down one flight of stairs, the sign above the entrance read The Resistance Room.

"What is this place? We know it is a museum but it looks so plush."

The woman answered, "Himmler wanted Ravensbruck to be his second home, this is a replica of the office in his home not far from here."

Everything was new and extremely elegant, all except a far wall. The flooring was a beautiful dark wood reflecting the old oak desk with a large picture hanging to the right side of it, a portrait of Adolf Hitler.

The woman waved us on saying, "Come. Come close." She walked over to a wall; it was cracked and partially destroyed by white paint and she said, "Careful stepping over the rope." It was a woven velvet dark blue rope separating the onlookers.

"What is this wall?" asked David, remembering what the psychic told him about a wall.

She said, "Look, closely," and flicked an overhead light on. You may have to come very close; it is very old."
They both walked up close to the wall and David ran his index finger over a black line then stepped back to see the entire painting.

"Is this what I think it is?"

"What is it?" said Daniel.

"Oh my god. Daniel Look. Do you see what this is?

Daniel looked up close, paused and said, "It's your painting. It is my sculpture.

They turned back, looked at the woman and then turned back and touched the wall as the woman said, "Your mother painted this."

They stood shocked and David asked, "When? When did she do this?"

The woman said, "Your mother was ordered to paint for Himmler by the commandant of the camp, Klaus Schuster. He was aware of your grandmother and he knew your mother was her daughter and he wanted her to paint for him, but, as you can imagine what happened, she was severely punished for it. She painted this behind another painting but Schuster found it. You see, your mother was a very strong woman and all she saw was the pain and suffering, even though she knew she was going to be punished for what she painted."
Daniel said, "I hope this is not as close as we are going to get to meet our mother? Is she still alive?"

The woman continued as if she hadn't heard the comment and said, "Your grandmother was very famous here in Germany and Poland and her paintings consisted of trees and landscapes, but your mother did paintings of the Jasper trees as well as one of a young man whom she was in love with as a young girl living in the ghettos. His name was Peter and he died in the Ghettos."

David asked, "Was Peter our father?"

The woman answered, "No."

"Do you know who our father is?" Daniel asked.

The woman paused and said, "No, no I do not know. I am so sorry. But we will take you to someone who knew your mother." There was silence before David asked, "So when are we going to meet her?"

"Today and all of your questions will be answered."

David and Daniel both kissed the wall where their mother last had her hand, then said, "This is amazing. Thank you so much for this." Then they both turned to the woman and said, "If this is all we will ever see of her, it will be enough. Thank you."

They walked up to her and kissed her cheek repeating, "Thank you, Gisela."

They went back into the vehicle and drove on, through small villages, tiny country lanes, passing town after town and driving for two and a half hours.

Finally Daniel said, "I'm so tired. I need to catch up on some sleep."

They both closed their eyes and went to sleep in the vehicle. When it had stopped they had arrived at a small cottage set back from the road. It had a cobblestone walkway, the garden was filled with bluebells, and they were lining the walkway. Two small lead glass windows were covered with English lavender vines and there was English lavender draped all over the windows. Ivy was trailing around the wooden planters that were also overgrown.
It was obvious it had been neglected, but it was also beautiful all the same.

They went up to the door and the woman walked in, and both David and Daniel followed. They both looked around. The front room was cluttered with nick knacks and antiques. There was an old rocking chair and on the wall behind it was an old-fashioned clock and next to that, an antique armoire with small photographs, some leaning against the back of the armoire and some set in fine frames.

Some were of children, others were of dogs, and several were of soldiers from the war. They continued through the lounge, turning the corner, and suddenly, in the far end of the extended room, there was a man, sitting in a padded print chair and he appeared to be very warm and comfortable by the gentle fire with a small black dog laying comfortably by his feet. He appeared to be very old and frail but his features were strong and boney, with high cheekbones and a bulbous nose. His features were deep with worry. He had a thin mouth and his eyes were small, hard to see under the thick untamed eyebrows, and he had thinning gray hair.

The woman walked up to his side and whispered, "They are here."

The man turned his head in the direction of where she was standing and the woman said to David and Daniel, "His eyesight is not very good, but it's enough for him to make you out."

Turning towards the boys, as if he knew of their whereabouts, the old man said in a weak, frail voice, "Please take a seat."

Daniel and David said, "Thank you sir."

They sat down in comfortable chairs, facing the fireplace as well as the old man and the woman who brought them there.

"Would you like some tea?" She asked.

David answered, "Yes tea would be wonderful."

Daniel replied also, "Yes please I'd love a cup of tea."

Daniel then asked, "What is your dog's name?"

The man answered, "His name is Fargo."

"May I pet him?"

"Yes, he's a good old dog, been my friend for years."

Daniel stroked the dog and the dog looked up, licked his hand and laid back down to enjoy the comfort of the fire and to be a comfort to his companion.

The old man then asked, "So what are your names?"

"I am Daniel."

"And I am David sir."

The man, looking in the other direction, said, "Good strong names. I like your names."

David said, "Sir, did you know our mother?"

The man paused; he picked up his cup of tea, caught by the surprise that his cup was empty and summoned Gisela.

"Yes sir." she said.

"May I have a refill on my tea?"

"Yes sir." She picked up his cup

He said, still looking toward the floor, "You are brothers?"

"Yes."

The woman brought the cup for the old man, followed with two cups of tea for the boys.

The old man went quiet again, picking up his fresh cup of tea, and shaking as he brought it to his thin lips. He took a sip and then, shaking, he placed the cup back into the saucer.

Daniel asked, "So did you know our mother?"

The old man said, "Yes, Yes, I did." He looked up. Her name brought a quiver to his lips as he whispered, "Christina. Christina. She was beautiful." He rested both hands on the arms of his chair, feeling the soft wood between his fingers.

Daniel looked at David as he asked, "What was she like?"

The man answered, "She was the most beautiful woman in the world." He shifted in his seat. It was obvious that the mention of her name made the old man uneasy and He continued, "A gifted woman, in my opinion the greatest artist in all of Germany, but she was never appreciated like she should have been."

"Did she ever talk about us?" Daniel asked.

The old man looked up, "Excuse me. Did you say something?"

Daniel asked again, 'Did our mother ever talk about us?"

"I am sorry," he apologized, "but my age has stolen many of my memories."

David, seeing the man was tiring and realizing he must be suffering severe dementia, said, "Tell us as much as you can about her."

"She was a free spirit. Like trying to harness the wind. You can't. She was strong."

Daniel asked, "Do you know if she is alive and where we might be able to see her?"

The man paused, he seemed confused, shook his head and said, "Please tell me what you just said?"

Daniel asked again, "Do you know where our mother is?"

The old man didn't answer, he just closed his eyes.

David tapped the knee of Daniel and looked at him and said, "It's enough. Mother is gone. We are never going to see her. I've come to that realization, that I'm never going to know, who my mother was and everything that I've gone through with the dreams and the memories. I'm just going to have to live with it. I want to leave. I know I said that I would be fine with just touching the wall that my mother painted, but I'm not. After hearing this man talk about her and hearing how wonderful she was, it just tears my heart out."

Daniel said, "But we have not talked to the woman who said she knew mother."

The woman, who brought them to the old man, had stayed out of the conversation, but she was observing and listening and then finally entered the room and said, "David, Daniel, Somebody else wants to meet you both."

They both looked at each other and she looked at the old man and they stood up. They began to walk down the hallway and as soon as they got out of hearing range, the old man said under his breath, "It was good to meet you, my sons."

They entered the darkened room and a small nightlight shined on an end table. A small framed person lay in the bed and the woman led them over to it and said, "She has been so excited to finally meet you, but she is very frail, and extremely weak. This is the lady who brought you here."

Daniel and David walked over to the bed, they looked at each other and a tiny hand reached out, touching David's hand and then Daniel's.

David said, "We have been to Ravensbruck and we have seen our mother's painting on the wall. We have been told you knew her. Is there anything you can share with us?"

She had a small face and said, in an almost inaudible voice, "I have been waiting my whole life to see you."

Daniel said, "So you must have been there when we were born!"

"Oh my...yes," she said and giggled.

David and Daniel both wondered if she too had dementia.

"I wanted to see you before I....leave. I was so frightened that I was never going to meet you."

David, almost afraid to ask, said, "Who are you, ma'am?"

"I am the one who painted the wall."

"No," Daniel said, "that can't be right, our mother painted it."

She said, "I am your Mother."

They immediately knelt down at the side of the bed, gently and sweetly embracing their mother and cried, "Mother we love you. We didn't know if you were alive."

Daniel kissed her hand as she stroked their hair, and said, "I am so glad we have found each other. My boys, my boys, my beautiful boys. The artist hand has brought you together. I prayed for this day."

She looked at them and then asked, "Is the artist in either of you?"

"Yes, yes mother. I am a painter, and Daniel is a Sculptor."

"I love you. I love you so much." She said as they felt her grip tighten then slowly released. She took in her last breath and then she was gone.

"Would it not be better to take my last breath here in the mud, a free woman than to return to a nazi hellhole, where people end up in a pile of bones...forgotten, or where burned flesh floats in the sky like snowflakes....?"

~Christina Nava~

ABOUT THE AUTHOR

Charlene Oliver has often been defined by "The song with a life of its own". Never Been To Me was first released in 1976. It was, by the standards of the day, ahead of its time. It reached #97 on the Billboard charts. When it was re-released in 1982 it climbed to #3 in the US and #1 in the UK where Paul McCartney and Stevie Wonder dominated the chart with Ebony and Ivory. By then Charlene had left Motown Records and was working in a sweet shop in England. The song was one of the biggest hits of that year. Nearly a decade later, it was featured as the opening song of the hit movie The Adventures of Priscilla, Queen of the Desert, which garnered her a large LGBT following. Last year Jimmy Fallon chose the song to perform on his hit TV show.
Charlene performing Never Been To Me in 1982:
http://youtu.be/SZgIk2b68gQ
Clip from the movie, The Adventures of Priscilla, Queen of the Desert:
http://youtu.be/suzwaW_SqtU
Jimmy Fallon singing Never Been To Me:
http://youtu.be/ImnL3QopFa0

Charlene released six albums all together but her creativity reached beyond music. She has written two books, her autobiography and a children's book. Now she has partnered with Olly Olly All In Free Productions to release her new Historical Fiction Novella "Orphan Train".

Made in the USA
Charleston, SC
28 July 2016